The
MAGNIFICENT
LIZZIE BROWN

and the

Ghost
Ship

D0309770

The
MAGNIFICENT
LIZZIE BROWN
and the
Ghost Ship

VICKI LOCKWOOD

Curious Fox CF

First published in 2015 by Curious Fox,
an imprint of Capstone Global Library Limited,
7 Pilgrim Street, London, EC4V 6LB
Registered company number: 6695582

www.curious-fox.com

Text © Hothouse Fiction Ltd 2015

Series created by Hothouse Fiction
www.hothousefiction.com

The author's moral rights are hereby asserted.

Cover illustration © Eva Morales 2015
Designed by Steve Mead

ISBN 978 1 78202 066 0

19 18 17 16 15
10 9 8 7 6 5 4 3 2 1

A CIP catalogue for this book is available from the British Library.

Typeset in Adobe Garamond Pro by Hothouse Fiction Ltd

Printed and bound by CPI Group (UK) Ltd, Croydon, CRO 4YY

With special thanks to
Adrian Bott

CHAPTER 1

Fitzy, who was both owner and ringmaster of the circus that bore his name, stood alone in the sawdust ring and lifted his gigantic hat to the audience.

'Ladies and gentlemen of Oxford – dear friends all – it has been a pleasure to entertain you for so many nights. But alas, all good things must come to an end.'

The audience sighed an *awwww*, but Fitzy dismissed it. 'No tears, I beg you. I ask only this: for one final time, please show your appreciation for the stars of our show, every one of them!' He brandished his cane. 'Maestro, please!'

As the band struck up a rum-tum-tiddly fanfare,

the various acts came prancing back into the ring. The coloured lights brightened, the audience cheered and clapped and Fitzy stood among it all, beaming like a lighthouse.

Nobody in the audience could see the two children who hid behind the beaded curtain, waving and grinning to their performer friends as they headed back out. One was Lizzie Brown, the circus's resident fortune-teller, who – unlike most sideshow psychics – genuinely had the ability to see into the future. The other was Fitzy's son Malachy, whose club foot couldn't slow down his razor-sharp mind.

'The Amazing Sullivan Sisters!' Fitzy announced.

Lizzie's best friends, the twins Erin and Nora, trotted past her on the backs of their flawless black horses, Albert and Victoria. Both girls had long red hair bound up in long plaits and fastened with silver brooches, and wore ballet dresses specially designed to be worn in the saddle.

Nora gave Lizzie a wave and wink. As they entered the ring, they stood up on their saddles, then tumbled over to stand on their hands. Lizzie watched, holding her breath with excitement, while the two girls entranced the audience once again.

Beside her, Malachy laughed. 'It's the same show they do every night. Aren't you tired of watching yet?'

'Never,' Lizzie said. How could she ever get tired of this? She was still new to the circus, true, but she knew the wonder of it all would never fade, no matter how much hard work needed to be done or how many early starts had to be endured. This brightly coloured world, always on the move, was where she belonged.

'Those merry masters of mayhem, the clowns!'

The clowns came charging past her in answer to Fitzy's call, but the moment they burst into the ring, they fell over, tumbling head-over-heels or slamming into one another. The audience roared with laughter. Lizzie smiled to see her friend JoJo chucking buckets of confetti about. Not long ago, he had been gravely ill with smallpox. Lizzie was happy to see that he was back to his old self.

'Good crowd tonight,' Malachy said, flipping a shiny shilling in his hand and catching it. 'Best pitch in a long time, this is.'

'I bet your dad's pleased.'

'Too right. After Kensal Green, this is just what he needed. He looks ten years younger, doesn't he?'

Lizzie shuddered at the memory of Kensal Green.

Setting up the circus so close to London's biggest cemetery hadn't worked out very well. All the animals had been skittish and the crowds slow in coming. Then Erin had been hurt too badly to perform, which meant no star turn and angry customers demanding refunds. And on top of all that, there had been the strange affair of the Devil's Hound… Everything had worked out in the end, thanks to the Penny Gaff Gang, but it had nearly bankrupted Fitzy.

'Thank heaven nothing's gone wrong here in Oxford,' she muttered. 'Not so far, anyway.'

She didn't tell Malachy, but that was her other reason for watching the show every night. It was becoming almost superstitious. She didn't dare miss it, in case something bad happened.

'The Astonishing Boissets!' Fitzy announced, hurling his cane up into the air.

The lights swivelled to reveal the high wire. The audience gasped as the family of French daredevils came trooping out onto it to take their bows. The wire trembled under their weight. Dru Boisset was in the centre – dark-haired, handsome and all of fourteen years old.

Lizzie's knuckles went to her mouth. No matter how

many times she saw their act, her nerves were always in knots. Even the presence of the safety net didn't help.

Malachy grinned. 'Do you think he can see you from up there?'

'Eh?' Lizzie glared at him.

'Does he know you watch him every night? Don't worry. I won't tell. But we both know why you're really here, Liz.'

'You cheeky little beggar!' Lizzie cried, storming towards him with her fist raised.

Malachy cringed away, laughing.

'Dru's just a friend and you know it,' Lizzie insisted. 'But I've seen *you* making puppy eyes at the twins!' *Sooner or later*, she thought, *I'll figure out which of the twins Mal has a crush on.*

'Whatever you say, mate.'

'One of these days I'll give you a fat lip,' Lizzie grumbled. She wasn't really angry, and Malachy was hardly the only one of her friends who teased her about Dru. But if she didn't lash out like this, they might realize that the sight of the boy really *did* make her insides go all fluttery.

Fitzy introduced the tumbling acrobats, then the boys of the Sullivan family came in riding their ponies, and lastly the stately elephants led by Hari, the Indian boy who was another of Lizzie's close friends. She was determined not to stare at Dru now, just to show Malachy, so she let her gaze rove over the audience instead.

They really were a well-to-do lot, this Oxford crowd. Men with top hats like a row of chimney pots, ladies with skin as pale as bone china, children in sailor suits and knickerbockers bouncing up and down in their seats. Lizzie guessed not one of those rosy-faced kids knew what it was like to go without a single meal, let alone face starvation.

She would have been jealous of children like that, back in the days when she lived in the London slum of Rat's Castle. They had lollipops and toys, while she had to struggle for a crust of bread. But her fortune-telling had taught her some surprising lessons. Even the richest of families could have terrible secrets, she now knew, and a pampered childhood didn't always mean happiness.

'Thank you once again, ladies and gentlemen, and good night!'

As Fitzy bowed, turned and bowed again, Lizzie noticed something strange in the front row. In the row of top hats, one of the heads was covered in bandages.

No, not bandages – a turban!

She could see the gentleman clearly now. 'Strewth,' she said, impressed. He was strikingly handsome, with dark skin like Hari's and elegantly cut clothes. Not shy of a bob or two, then. And were those jewelled rings on his fingers?

The English people beside him were clapping politely, but the stylish gentleman was showing no such restraint. '*Bravo!*' he shouted, applauding wildly. '*Encore!*'

Lizzie grinned to see an adult enjoying himself so much. Usually, only children would react with this kind of wild excitement. Either this man didn't realize it wasn't quite proper to go overboard like this, or he didn't care. Nobody was shushing him, at any rate. Maybe they didn't dare to.

The lady sitting next to him was smiling and looking at him fondly. Was she his wife? She was blonde and beautiful, like a painting from the top of a tin of chocolates. Lizzie thought she must have seen her somewhere before, in the papers, maybe. She looked like a society lady, or perhaps an actress or a foreign princess. She held a broad fan with peacock feathers, slowly fanning herself, and Lizzie was reminded of the way a cat's tail will sometimes lash slowly, when it's sitting and thinking.

Then *the feeling* was upon her, gripping her whole body as suddenly as a sneeze and every bit as impossible to control. Lizzie let out a tiny gasp, and then stood stock-still as the pictures began to appear in her mind.

I'm having one of me visions! she thought, fearful and excited at once. Most of the time, her visions appeared when she was doing readings for people, but they sometimes struck out of the blue, just like this one. They were much stronger than the others, and they always warned of trouble to come...

She saw herself outside, at night, somewhere cold. She was standing in a curved archway. Reaching out to touch the sides of the arch, she realized that it was made of bone.

Moving in slow motion, she passed through the arch and found herself overlooking the sea. She was standing at the top of a rocky cliff, breathing the salt air and hearing the cries of the gulls. There was something haunted about this place.

She saw a tidy seaside village below, buildings clustered on the sides of a dip in the land, a ruin on a cliff ... and out at sea, but drawing closer, a ship surrounded by mist like something out of a ghost story. A strange green light shone from it...

Someone was poking her hard in the arm. Malachy. She blinked, coming back to herself.

'You OK?' he asked, sounding doubtful.

Lizzie shuddered and blew air out – *phew!* 'I had a vision. It wasn't a blurry one, so I know it wasn't the past. It was clear, so it must have been showing me the future.'

'Was there a crime going on?' Malachy was suddenly excited, and with good reason. Lizzie's visions had predicted crimes before, crimes that their circle of friends – the Penny Gaff Gang, as they had named themselves – had managed to stop.

'No,' said Lizzie, puzzled. 'I was at the seaside. At least I think I was.'

'Eh?'

'I've never even seen the sea before. But there was such a lot of water, it had to be the sea. And a town, and bones, and this weird ship in a cloud of mist.'

'The seaside.' Malachy laughed. 'Reckon you're losing your touch, mate. We're off to Reading next. There's no beaches there! No jellied eels, neither!'

'Reading? But it was so clear!'

Lizzie had never considered what would happen if her powers abandoned her, or worse, led her wrongly. She'd just be a crazy girl then, fit only for the lunatic asylum.

After the show, the circus folk all packed into the tea tent for the traditional last night party. There was wine for the adults, watered beer or lemonade for the kids, and cake for everyone. Lizzie grinned to see Rice Pudding Pete, the messiest of the clowns, nibble daintily at his cake as if he were a dowager countess.

'Where's Fitzy?' asked Nora through a mouthful of crumbs.

'He went off to have a word in private,' Ma Sullivan told her with a knowing look.

'With who?'

'A person of considerable means. That's all I'm saying.'

Lizzie was certain she knew who Fitzy was talking to. 'It was that chap with the turban, wasn't it?'

'Reckon you'll all find out soon enough.'

As it turned out, they only had to wait a few seconds.

Fitzy strolled into the tea tent with the turbaned gentleman by his side, beaming at the crowd.

'If I could have your attention for a moment? This, my friends, is Maharaja Gurinder Bhatti.'

Lizzie and Nora looked at one another, open-mouthed. 'A maharaja? That's like a bloomin' king or something!' whispered Lizzie.

'Lovely to meet you all,' the Maharaja said, with just a hint of an Indian accent. 'May I?' He helped himself to a piece of cake and made a face as if he had just tasted heaven. 'Mmm. This is wonderful.'

Ma Sullivan giggled like a schoolgirl, and seemed suddenly unable to speak a word.

'The Maharaja has told me how much he enjoyed our little show tonight,' Fitzy said. 'I am delighted to tell you that we've been invited to put on a special performance—'

'Please be my guests in Whitby,' the Maharaja interrupted eagerly. 'I've just taken the lease on Dunsley Castle, and I think my new neighbours in the town would love a circus.'

'Naturally, I have accepted. We can hardly refuse a royal command!' Fitzy told the stunned crowd.

'Please. It is a request, no more.'

'Your Majesty, your merest request is our command. Next weekend, we shall be in Whitby to entertain the locals. Now, Maharaja, a glass of champagne?'

As the drinks were poured, everyone broke into excited conversation.

'Where's Whitby?' Lizzie asked Malachy.

Malachy said nothing.

'Why are you lookin' at me like that?'

'Whitby's in North Yorkshire. It's a seaside town.' Malachy sighed. 'I know, I know. We're going to the seaside after all. You saw it coming. When will I learn? Your visions are never wrong, are they?'

'Not so far,' Lizzie laughed, relieved.

Anita, billed as the World's Smallest Woman, seemed less thrilled than everyone else. 'It's very kind of the Maharaja, I'm sure, but it'll take us a dog's age to get up to Whitby. Plodding along in our old horse-drawn carts is all very well, but we'll be on the road for a week!'

'I think you may find it takes a good deal less time than that,' Fitzy said.

Anita folded her arms and snorted. 'Oh? What you got in mind, Fitzy? A flying carpet?'

But Fitzy's only answer was a secretive smile.

CHAPTER 2

Lizzie stood on the train platform and swallowed. The train loomed before her, a mechanical beast, its smoke stack belching vapour and its pistons like metal bones. Steam hissed around Lizzie's ankles like dragon breath. Now that she actually had to get *on* it, the prospect of her first ever train journey was more terrifying than exciting.

'Come on, Lizzie!' called Nora and Erin together, sticking their heads out of the train window.

'If you don't get on the train, you'll have to walk,' Nora shouted.

'And it's a long way to Whitby!' added Erin.

All around Lizzie, the circus people were climbing on board, chatting excitedly and hauling bulging bags. Many of them were waving out of the windows, shouting to late arrivals to hurry up.

Lizzie just stood as if she'd been turned to stone. She stared at the gap between the station platform and the carriage. *People must fall down there all the time*, she imagined. *They must get sliced to pieces by those huge iron wheels.*

Malachy was already on board. 'The Maharaja's hired a whole train, just for us! Isn't it marvellous?' he'd said to her, just before barging past everyone else in a mad scramble to be one of the first on board. Well, Lizzie didn't think it was marvellous. It was a monstrous thing, this locomotive, hissing and clanking, and stinking of scorched metal like an iron left too long in the fire.

'They explode, they do,' Lizzie muttered to herself. 'I've read it in the papers. The boilers go bang. Terrible tragedy. Hundreds dead.'

'Lizzie, come *on*! You'll miss it!'

'I'll just be a minute,' she shouted to Nora.

She took a deep breath, counted to three and took a single bold step towards the train. Just then, the whistle went off with a sound like a screaming banshee and the smoke stack let out a belch of white steam. Lizzie squealed in horror and scrambled back away from it. She sat down on a bench, panting heavily.

Dru sauntered past, wearing a frock coat and looking every inch the young gentleman. He either hadn't seen her or was pretending he hadn't, but either way he suddenly stopped in his tracks and turned to her with a smile. 'Ah, Lizzie. This is your first time on a train, *n'est-ce pas?*'

'It will be, if I ever get on the bloomin' thing.'

Dru crossed the platform, stepped onto the train and held out his hand. 'Come, *ma chère amie*. Do not worry. I will protect you.'

Without a second thought, Lizzie stormed towards him. She ignored his hand and left it hanging in the air as she stepped up, pushed past him and threw herself into the carriage. She flopped down into the nearest seat, alongside Nora and Erin who squealed with glee.

Dru followed her into the carriage and raised an eyebrow at Lizzie. 'Girls,' he said with a shrug. 'Always contradictory.'

'It's only a train,' Lizzie scoffed. Her heart was hammering as she smoothed down her skirt and crossed her legs. Then she uncrossed them and sat her bag on her lap. How were you supposed to sit in a train carriage, anyway?

A station guard waved a flag and blew a quick *peep-peep* on his whistle. Erin grinned at her. 'We'll start moving any minute!'

'We'll be in Yorkshire tomorrow morning, just one day after we left Oxford,' Nora said. 'I can't believe it. It's magic. Like something out of *Tales of the Arabian Nights*.'

'The Maharaja isn't Arabian,' Dru said. 'He's Indian.'

'He's rich is what he is!' said Erin, laughing. 'And he knows exactly what to do with his money. When I'm rich, I'll hire whole trains for my friends to ride around in too.'

The train lurched forwards.

'Oh Gawd!' Lizzie gasped, frantically grabbing her seat. 'Oh blimey. Make 'em stop. I've got to get off.'

'Don't be daft, Lizzie,' said Nora. 'Relax. Enjoy the ride.'

'Enjoy the ride?' Lizzie repeated as if Nora had told her to eat a tasty frog. 'You're barmy. Oh Gawd, we're going even faster!'

'We haven't even left the station,' Dru pointed out.

Lizzie covered her face and moaned. She stayed that

way for a whole minute. Then she asked, 'Are we in Yorkshire yet?'

'Lizzie, seriously now, calm down,' Nora said, putting an arm around Lizzie's shoulders. 'We'll be on this train for a good few hours to come, so you'd best get used to it and stop acting the cod.'

Lizzie slowly lowered her hands. She looked out of the window and caught a last glimpse of the train station. She desperately wished she was plodding along on her shabby caravan, which she'd taken to calling Old Jemima.

'It can't be safe,' she whispered. 'It just can't. God didn't mean for us to go this fast. It ain't natural.'

She gripped her seat and stayed clamped there like a crab as the train chugged out of Oxford and picked up speed. Town buildings gave way to green fields and hedgerows as the countryside volleyed past. At first Lizzie felt like she was trapped on a carriage pulled by mad runaway horses, but after a while she started getting used to the sensation. Her fingers gradually relaxed their grip, her breathing slowed down and her heart stopped trying to batter its way out of her ribcage.

Cows and sheep shot past the window. Not enough

time to count them. From across the rattling, swaying carriage, Dru gave her a smile.

Malachy and Hari appeared at the door to their compartment. 'Guess who's been up the front with the driver?' Malachy said proudly.

'Rather you than me,' Lizzie muttered.

Malachy ignored her. 'He reckons I'm a natural!'

'Just in time for a picnic, Mal, now the gang's all here,' Nora said. She and Erin unpacked a wicker basket, laying out sandwiches, sausages, an Irish potato dish called 'colcannon' made with spring onions and cream, and the remains of last night's cake.

'You go ahead,' Malachy said. 'I need to check Dad's accounts.' He opened a fat ledger and ran his finger down the columns of figures, muttering sums to himself.

The Penny Gaff Gang eagerly tucked in, and somewhere in the middle of her third slice of cake, Lizzie somehow forgot all about being scared of the train.

'Your mum makes the best cake in the world,' she said, licking her fingers.

'This isn't even her best!' Erin said. 'Just you wait until our birthday. The cake she makes then ... oh, you'll die. Of pure pleasure!'

'Just over a week to go!' Nora said, her voice rising to an excited squeak.

'The day after the big Whitby show,' said Erin. 'So don't go making any big plans, because there's going to be a party, and of course you're invited.'

'When's your birthday?' Nora asked, turning to Lizzie. 'We need to throw you a party.'

'Maybe she doesn't like parties,' Erin threw in.

'Don't be daft. Everyone likes parties. Or maybe there's something you do instead? Something special?' Nora continued, still looking at Lizzie.

Erin eyed her friend askance. 'What *do* you do on your birthday?'

'Don't do anything,' Lizzie said with a sigh.

'What?' the twins said, horrified.

'Back in Rat's Castle, nobody cared about birthdays. They were just like any other day. I've never even been to a birthday party, let alone had one of my own.'

Erin and Nora looked shocked, then hugged her, one on each side. 'We're going to do something about that,' Nora said. 'Aren't we, Erin?'

'That's right.'

The narrow streets and mean, grimy rooms of

London's Rat's Castle slum were a long way away now. Sometimes, in her dreams, Lizzie would think she was back there. Pa would loom over her again, his breath stinking of beer and his rough fists brandished in her face. It had been a hungry, frightened life for a young girl, with no hope in sight. There were plenty of children still there, trapped behind the cracked, grimy windows.

Then salvation had come, parading through the streets in gold and glitter – Fitzy's Travelling Circus, filled with the most marvellous, unusual people Lizzie had ever known. Back then, people like the Amazon Queen and the World's Smallest Woman had been things of wonder to Lizzie. Now they were her friends.

I'll always be in Fitzy's debt, she thought to herself. *He took me on before I showed any sign of having psychic powers, just out of the goodness of his heart.*

Suddenly Fitzy was there in person, poking his head round their compartment door and grinning just like Malachy. 'Everyone enjoying the ride?'

'It's fantastic!' Malachy yelled.

'Smashing!' said Nora and Erin together.

Dru shrugged and stretched his strong arms over his head. 'It's a very relaxing way to travel, Fitzy. I might even take a *petit* nap.'

'And you, Lizzie?'

Lizzie smiled weakly. 'Didn't fancy it at first, but I'm getting used to it.'

'We're on the road to riches, my young friends,' Fitzy said, rubbing his hands together. 'A royal command performance! Did you all know the Maharaja is one of Queen Victoria's favourites? Hopefully he'll tell all his rich friends about our circus.' He rubbed the fabric of the seat cushions and smiled approvingly. 'If the cash keeps coming in like this, we can buy a train of our own. A circus train. The first of its kind in the country.'

Malachy looked up from the accounts ledger. 'Don't get ahead of yourself, Dad.'

'*Woo woo!*' cried Fitzy, tooting an imaginary train whistle. 'Oh, Hari, I nearly forgot. Your uncle Zezete needs your help back in the animal carriage.'

Hari leaped to his feet. 'Are the animals all right?'

'Oh, none of them are hurt. They're just not getting into the spirit of the train ride like you young things are.'

'They're scared,' Hari said, quickly swallowing his last bite of cake. 'I'll be right there.'

Lizzie felt a pang. Poor animals – they didn't

understand what was happening to them. They weren't used to the strange smells and horrible noises, and the rocking and swaying about. She knew exactly how they felt.

'Hang on, Hari,' she called after him. 'I'll come too.'

Akula the elephant lay on her side in the straw. Her legs twitched and kicked erratically, like a dog dreaming of chasing rabbits. Her eyes were full of fear and her body trembled as if she were freezing cold.

'She's petrified!' Lizzie said. 'We've got to do something!'

'Keep your voice down,' Hari told her. She knew he wasn't angry; he was just letting her know how best to calm the elephant. Hari knelt down by Akula's huge head and stroked her trunk gently. 'There now, my lovely. Calm now. All's well.'

'What can I do?'

'Stroke her ears, slowly. She likes that.'

Together, they soothed Akula. Hari sang Indian songs, weaving melodies that sounded strange and beautiful to Lizzie. All the notes went up and down like fireflies dancing. She didn't understand a word, of course, but the syllables were softly enchanting, with the dark beauty of peacock feathers and gleaming jewels.

When Zezete came in, bringing a bucket of feed, he said nothing at first. He squatted down and watched her and Hari at work together. When Akula fell into a happy sleep, he smiled.

'You have a real gift for working with the elephants, Lizzie,' he said. 'If you ever grow tired of being the circus's fortune-teller, you can always join us as an animal handler.'

'I like the songs you were singing,' she told Hari. 'Are they from India?'

'No, Lizzie,' Hari said, his face very serious. 'They are from the moon.'

Lizzie stared, then cracked up laughing. 'Ask a silly question! So ... do you two know anything about the Maharaja, then? He's Indian, isn't he? Fitzy says he's one of Queen Victoria's favourites!'

Zezete spat on the floor and muttered something harsh-sounding. He wasn't speaking English. Hari glanced nervously at his uncle, then looked down. Lizzie had the creeping feeling that she'd said something foolish.

'I need to feed the camels,' Zezete said, in English this time. His voice was colder than Lizzie had ever heard it before. Next second, he was gone without a backward glance.

'Hari, I didn't mean—'

'I know,' Hari interrupted. 'He knows too. He won't be angry with you. But you'd best let him cool off.'

'What did I do?'

Hari sighed. 'It's a long story. Ugly too. You're sure you want to hear it?'

'Yes!'

They leaned against Akula's back as she slept, while Hari patiently explained.

'Gurinder Bhatti may be the latest society favourite here in England, but to us Indians he's a traitor. He was a prince of Punjab, but he sold his country to the British East India company.'

Lizzie struggled to imagine selling a whole country to a foreign power.

'He gave England the Khyber Diamond too. All that stuff your queen says about India being the jewel in her crown? That jewel's stolen property, and the likes of Gurinder Bhatti are responsible.'

'But … he seemed so nice.' Lizzie could hardly believe the jolly man had betrayed millions of Indians, all for money.

'Oh, he knows how to play the part of the dashing prince,' Hari said sourly. 'He's handsome and wealthy, the toast of British high society and friends with Queen Victoria, but he's not exactly popular back home!'

CHAPTER 3

Lizzie woke up in straw-smelling darkness. She was still lying against Akula's warm, heaving flank. She must have dozed off, she realized. *Not the smartest thing in the world, falling asleep curled up with an elephant. What if she* had *rolled over in the night and flattened me?*

Silly. Akula would never do that. Lizzie felt safe around the huge animal, even when she was asleep. She felt round until she found Akula's head, gave it a fond pat, then stood up and brushed the straw from her dress.

What time was it, she wondered? The train was still rattling along. She opened the door to the next carriage, letting in the grey light of morning, and groped her way blearily through the train until she found her own place.

Her friends were all where they'd left them, but now they were slumped snoring in their seats. Dru had propped his feet on the seats opposite, Malachy was using the ledger as a pillow, and Erin and Nora were clutching each other as if they feared to be parted.

Lizzie stepped over Dru's legs. She watched him sleep for a moment, then felt funny about it and settled into her own empty seat by the window. Nobody woke up.

She didn't mind the speed of the train at all now. Odd how quickly you could get used to new things. Through the window, she watched the sun rise over wide, rolling countryside, much of it empty and rugged but beautiful with it. She saw dry stone walls, sheep nestled into the grass, rocky rough slopes and great acres of desolate moorland. The cottages were stony and small, like holdovers from some earlier part of history.

Malachy stirred and opened his eyes. 'Morning,' he mumbled. Yawning, he asked, 'Where are we?'

'Somewhere with a lot of moors.'

'We must be in North Yorkshire! Yes – see that river down there, all silvery and twisting like it was made of molten metal? That's the River Esk. It flows down to the sea at Whitby.'

Lizzie clenched her hands together with excitement. 'We're almost there!'

Her loud voice woke up the others. Sleepiness soon vanished like morning dew as they realized how close to Whitby they were. Suddenly the last few miles of the journey seemed like the longest of all.

Lizzie couldn't stop staring at the river. It meant the seaside was close. Ever since she was little, she'd dreamed of going to the beach one day. The closest she'd ever come was the muddy banks of the Thames.

Out on the moors, people were leading ponies laden with packs. 'What are they doing up so early?' she wondered aloud. 'They can't be farmers.'

'They're bringing rough jet home from the coast,' Malachy told her. 'You know what jet is, don't you?'

'Something … black? 'Cause people say "jet black", don't they?'

'That's right. It's a shiny black stone. That's what's in those packs. Cracking great lumps of rough jet.'

'And the Whitby jewellers make it into brooches,

bracelets, rings and necklaces,' Nora cut in. 'It's beautiful stuff.'

Malachy chuckled. 'Funny to think of fine ladies wearing jewellery made from fossilized trees. That's what jet is, you know.'

'Malachy!'

'Like wearing coal, really … ow! Nora, stop kicking me!'

The last leg of the journey was on the road. The brightly coloured circus caravans, which had been securely tied onto flat goods wagons, were now wheeled down ramps with loving care and reunited with their horses and ponies. It was only a few miles to travel, and the battlements of Dunsley Castle were soon in view over the treetops.

'It's a real castle!' Lizzie gasped, standing up on the roof of her caravan. Her old home had been called 'Rat's Castle' as a bitter joke. What would the people back there say if they could see her now?

'Fit for a princess!' Malachy called across.

'It's so funny, suddenly being here,' Lizzie said

dreamily. 'Seems like no time's passed at all. Like a giant scooped up the whole circus, caravans and all, and plonked us down here in the north.'

'Smell that salt air?' Hari took a deep breath. 'You can tell we're close to the sea.'

'I can't wait!' The palms of Lizzie's hands itched with anticipation.

'You're going to have to wait,' Malachy reminded her. 'We all are. Can't go running off until the tents are all pitched.'

That brought her back down to earth with a bump. 'Sometimes, Mal, you really remind me of your dad.'

But Lizzie wasn't workshy. From the moment the caravan convoy pulled up on the gravel forecourt of Dunsley Castle, she threw herself into the work along with the rest of the company. For the next three hours, she helped to unroll huge sheets of canvas, haul bundles of poles in multiple sections, pound thick tent pegs into the ground and unload endless boxes of props and costumes.

The grassy lawns were thick and lush, the finest she'd ever seen. The flowerbeds nearby were peppered with blooms. Bashing stakes into the ground felt a little bit like vandalism, but this was where the Maharaja wanted them to perform, so this was where the tents would be pitched. *After all,* Lizzie thought, *it's his garden and he can do what he wants with it.*

She and Dru worked their way around the outside of the tea tent, Dru holding the stakes in place and Lizzie walloping them with a mallet. She couldn't take her eyes off the stunning castle behind them; with its parapets and towers it looked like something from medieval times.

It wasn't that old, she knew; most of the really old castles were nothing but ruins now. And Dunsley Castle was really just a manor house, done up to look like a castle. Even so, she could imagine princesses walking along the battlements, their long silken dresses fluttering in a warm summer's breeze…

Lost in her dreams, she swung and missed the stake completely. The mallet whacked into the grass, gouging out a chunk of earth. Dru sprang away with an acrobat's reflexes.

'Lizzie, watch what you're doing *s'il vous plaît!*'

'Sorry!' She folded her arms and leaned on the mallet handle. 'It's just that I think I've fallen in love with that house.'

'An Englishman's home is his castle,' Dru teased.

'Maybe an English*woman*'s too.'

Lizzie just snorted at that. She lifted the mallet, and Dru went back to work with a merry whistle.

By mid-afternoon, the red and white striped show tent was in place, towering over all the smaller tents. To one side a staked-out corral enclosed the circus ponies, who were munching the lush grass happily. They seemed none the worse after their long journey on the train, Lizzie was glad to see. Erin, Nora and the other Sullivan siblings – Patrick and Sean, Brendan and Conor – sat on the grass beside them on a blanket, enjoying yet another picnic.

As Lizzie bashed in the last of the pegs, a furious yell resounded from the castle. 'Oi!' came the shout, and then again, '*Oi!*'

Dru looked up, puzzled. 'The Maharaja?'

'Didn't sound like him.'

It wasn't. The man running towards them was white, hefty and wore moleskin britches with braces, a neckerchief and a cap. His whiskers were greying and a huge wart protruded from the side of his nose. *He looks like a sprouting potato*, thought Lizzie, *lumpy and grubby*. He carried a spade over his shoulder like a slung musket.

He glared at Lizzie as he passed, then carried on until he reached the Sullivans. 'What the 'ell do you mean by letting your animals rove on this 'ere grass?' From the way he pronounced 'grass' to rhyme with 'lass', Lizzie knew he had to be a local man. 'Are you aware you're trespassin' on private property?'

Nora burst out, 'We was only—'

'Irish, is it? We don't want no gypsy freeloaders round 'ere. You'd better move on before I start movin' yer.'

To prove he meant it, he held the shovel like a club, menacing Sean with it and Lizzie felt a cold fear that the young man would jump to his feet and knock the older man out cold. His sisters were being threatened, and Sean never allowed that.

But he kept his cool, thank heavens. 'I don't believe we've been introduced,' he said with smooth good manners. 'We're the Sullivans. It's a pleasure to meet you. And you are?'

'My name's Johnson, you cheeky bleeder!' roared the man. Lizzie couldn't tell whether it was Sean's cocky attitude that had set him off, or his refusal to be intimidated. 'These are my gardens your horses are chewing up!'

'Aren't they the Maharaja's gardens?' said Erin, acting unruffled, taking her cue from Sean. 'Cucumber sandwich, Mister Johnson?'

'You can stuff your ruddy sandwiches,' Johnson yelled, purple in the face now. *More like a beetroot than a potato*, Lizzie thought. He lurched forwards as if he really meant to hit someone with his spade.

Hari came running over. 'What's the matter? Why all the shouting?'

Johnson rolled his eyes at the sight of Hari. 'That's all we bloomin' need. Another one.'

'Another what?'

Johnson didn't answer the question. 'I'm the gardener here at Dunsley Castle, I'll have you know. Do you lot have any idea how much work it takes to keep these gardens immaculate? And here you come, loosing horses on 'em, banging stakes in, heaven knows what else!' A sneer came over his face. 'You've probably got bloomin' elephants in them tents, haven't you?'

'Two, actually,' Hari said. His white teeth gleamed as he smiled broadly. 'I'm very proud of them.'

When he realized that Hari was serious, Johnson's face went through several amazing contortions. He looked as though he was having a heart attack.

'We do have every right to be here, Mister Johnson,' Hari said politely. 'We're invited guests of the Maharaja. We're not squatters.'

Johnson's voice went very quiet. 'You don't belong here,' he hissed. 'When it all blows up in your faces – and it will – don't say I didn't warn you.'

'This is gettin' out of hand,' Lizzie told Dru. 'Let's get Fitzy before someone gets hurt.'

But the ringmaster was already hurrying over, with Malachy close behind. 'Mister Johnson, I'm so sorry. You should have been notified of our arrival. The message must have gone astray.'

'You've turned these grounds into a farmyard,' Johnson raved. 'This place has been tended for hundreds of years, and you lot come rolling in and treat it like a public park! I'll be making a formal complaint to his nibs about this.'

'I promise you, on my word of honour, that we'll be respectful of the grounds.' Fitzy's voice had a calm authority that even the gardener couldn't deny. All his ranting and bluster suddenly looked ridiculous next to Fitzy's mannerly goodwill. He fidgeted like a schoolboy caught throwing paper darts.

Lizzie was quietly impressed. Fitzy was surely as

exhausted as everyone else, but he was still the solid rock on which the whole circus rested.

Johnson shrank into himself like a toad. He glanced about, finally letting his gaze rest on Hari. 'You people...' he muttered, adding something Lizzie couldn't hear, but which sounded obscene. 'Him too. He'll be sorry. There's an evil wind coming, you mark me. And when the Devil sails into Whitby harbour on his ghost ship, he'll find no shortage of sinners to carry off!' With that, he stomped off towards the castle, lifting his legs high with each step as if he were wading through mud.

'Ghost ship?' said Nora, looking worried.

'He's just trying to scare us with superstitious nonsense,' Lizzie said firmly. But in the back of her mind, she remembered the ghostly green ship she'd seen in her vision. Could the groundskeeper be right, she wondered. Had she foreseen the Devil sailing into Whitby harbour?

'What an unpleasant little man,' Fitzy said, holding his chin thoughtfully. Then he shrugged, as if the matter was already forgotten. 'Best move the horses around, folks. Not too much grazing in any one place, savvy?'

'Right you are,' Erin said with a salute. Fitzy went

to inspect the big top, while Malachy lingered to help finish off the picnic.

Lizzie was still watching Johnson dwindle into the distance, leaving a trail of swear words hanging on the air. 'What's the matter with him, anyway?' she wondered aloud. 'The Maharaja's giving the locals a circus for free, isn't he? You'd think he'd be happy, not starting up like ... like an angry badger!'

'Think about it, Liz,' Malachy said, digging the last of the jam out of the pot with a finger. 'The locals probably didn't like the Maharaja from the start. That's why he's giving them a circus. To try and win them over.'

'But ... he's rich, he's popular, why would the people here hate him?'

Malachy and Hari exchanged a glance. Suddenly the penny dropped. 'Oh,' Lizzie said. 'Oh. It's because he's foreign, isn't it?'

'Foreign and brown,' Hari said, in tones that hurt Lizzie's heart. 'You heard what he said to me. "Another one." I'm not even from the Punjab. I'm from Goa.'

'Not every community opens its arms as readily as Fitzy's circus,' Malachy said sadly. 'Some people just hate anyone who's different from them.'

Lizzie thought how much wealth the Maharaja would bring to this town. 'Even if they've got loads of money?'

Malachy looked sour. 'Especially if they've got loads of money. It's even easier to hate someone you're jealous of.'

CHAPTER 4

'Come in,' said Fitzy, in answer to the knock on his caravan door.

'The tents are all up,' Lizzie said breathlessly. The rest of the Penny Gaff Gang waited behind her, as eager as she was. 'Hari's seen to the animals, and everyone's settled in all right, so…'

'Hmm,' Fitzy said, turning to face her. 'And I suppose you lot want to go gadding off into town now all the hard work's done, do you?'

'Please,' Lizzie said, biting her lip.

Fitzy gave her a hard stare, then broke into a wide grin. 'Of course you can. Off you go.' They were already sprinting away when he added, 'Enjoy yourselves. *But—*'

Fitzy's 'but' stopped them all in their tracks like dogs suddenly coming to the ends of their leashes. Lizzie, yearning to leave, turned to see what more he could possibly want.

Fitzy passed her a thick stack of handbills and a pot of paste. 'Make yourselves useful while you're there,' he said. 'I want posters up wherever there's empty space, you understand? Be polite, it costs nothing. Ask in the shops if they'll stick one up in the window or by the door. But none on any private property without the owner's permission, and for heaven's sake don't stick 'em on any churches or memorials or stuff like that. We've already had one angry local giving us a piece of his mind.'

'He had precious few pieces left to give if you ask me,' Malachy said, making the others laugh.

Fitzy smiled too, despite himself. 'Just mind your manners, understood?'

'What about selling tickets?' Lizzie asked. It was part of the usual routine when they arrived in a new town and she was good at it.

Fitzy knocked gently on the top of her head with his

knuckles, as if he was expecting a hollow sound. 'It's a free show, remember? Our good friend the Maharaja's footing the bill.'

Lizzie rolled her eyes. She took off after the others, who were already running across the grass. 'Careful of the lawn!' Fitzy bellowed. 'And be back here by six or there'll be hell to pay!'

The walk back into Whitby led along a coastal road. Lizzie's first sight of the sea, so huge and broad and glittering, made her stomach clench with nervous excitement 'It's the sea,' she whispered. 'It's really the sea...'

'Blimey,' said Malachy, 'so it is.'

The sight of the light dancing on the water was a beautiful agony to Lizzie. The sea had woken a strange, deep, aching hunger in her. She feared it, and yet she craved it at the same time.

Back in Kensal Green, she'd nearly drowned in the Grand Union canal. People from Rat's Castle rarely knew how to swim unless they were sailors. Since then, she'd been wary of the water.

'We should make a plan,' Malachy said. 'Figure out who wants to do what.'

'Look in the shops,' said Erin and Nora together.

'Hunt for fossils on the beach,' said Hari.

Dru just shrugged. 'I don't mind. Whatever the girls want to do.'

'And you, Lizzie?'

'I want to sit on the beach,' she said firmly. She could always watch the sea from a safe spot, and maybe paddle in it if she felt brave enough.

'Well then.' Malachy began a determined stride forward. 'We'd better get going.'

The town of Whitby lay on sloping land that ran down to the river. The roads wove back and forth, sometimes doubling back on each other like a mountain pass, sometimes driving steeply downhill towards the water. The buildings were all at different heights, lying at different levels on the slopes. From a distance, it looked as if you could jump from the higher roofs to the lower ones.

Lizzie saw the whalebone arch from her vision at the top of the west cliff. On the opposite side of the bay, high on the eastern cliff, was the stone ruin she'd seen. That, she now knew, was Whitby Abbey. Even in this bright daylight, it seemed lonely and faintly sinister. There was no sign of the strange fog-shrouded ship.

Suddenly, Johnson's words came back to her. '*When the Devil sails into Whitby harbour…*' And just like that, she knew with a cold certainty that there was mystery here, something dark and unspoken that hovered over the town like a mist.

Lizzie badly wanted to run down the steep steps to the beach, but she knew they had work to do first. There were posters to put up and goodwill to spread. They strolled along the main shopping street, sticking up posters wherever they could.

The jewellers in the main street was called Delingpole's. The windows were stocked with sparkling jet, black and shiny as molasses. Lizzie hadn't seen it close up before, and she pressed her nose to the glass along with Erin and Nora.

'Queen Victoria really wears this?' she said. It was beautiful, dark but glossy, fashioned into beads both smooth and faceted, into oval brooches, teardrops and even delicately carved cameos showing ladies' faces in profile. 'It's like black amber.'

Nora groaned theatrically. 'I want it all. It's so beautiful. Dark and mysterious. I'd love to be dripping with jet, I would.'

'Hard to believe it was all just lying there buried in the ground.' Hari seemed fascinated, to Lizzie's surprise. 'Buried treasure.'

'That necklace!' Nora jabbed her finger at a necklace like a waterfall of black droplets, draped over a velvet cloth.

Lizzie looked at her friend's pale skin and red hair. 'You've got just the right colouring for black jewellery,' she said.

Hari nodded.

'Well, you have got a birthday coming up,' teased Erin. 'We'll have to see what we can do. Wait, Lizzie, stop!'

The bell on the door dinged loudly. The man behind the counter eyed Lizzie as she pushed her way in. 'Anything I can help you with, love?'

Lizzie handed him a circus poster. 'Stick that in your door?'

'Do I get free tickets if I do?'

'Don't need any. It's a free show.' Lizzie hummed

casually and strolled over to the window display. She tried to put on a posh voice. 'I say, that's a handsome necklace there.'

'You like it?' the shopkeeper said with a slight smile.

'Might I ask the price?'

He told her.

Spluttering, pale with shock, Lizzie pushed her way out of the shop without another word. 'Don't ask,' she gasped to her startled friends outside. 'Just don't ask. Let's just go to the beach.'

The sun was lower in the sky by the time they finally reached the beach. There were still bathers all along its length; the women in one group, the men in another further down. Lizzie stared at the strange wheeled huts that some of the bathers were using.

'They're bathing machines,' Erin explained. 'You can't have rich ladies getting changed and taking a dip in front of everyone, can you? Wouldn't be proper. So they hide inside those things.'

'Are we going to get in trouble if we go in together?' Lizzie looked nervously at Hari, Malachy and Dru.

'Maybe the boys had better go down the other end.'

Nora let out a *pfff* of scorn. 'Leave all that foolishness to the grown-ups. Nobody's going to say anything to a bunch of kids.'

'I hope not,' Lizzie shuddered, glancing around in case a policeman or some other guardian of public morality was standing watch.

With nowhere else to change and no money for a bathing machine, they stood around in a circle facing outwards and took it in turns to put their costumes on in the middle. Some of the posh ladies stared, but Nora and Erin stared back until they lost their nerve.

I don't even have a bathing suit, Lizzie thought dismally. She'd just have to hitch up her skirts and paddle.

Finally the two Sullivan girls stood in their glory, ready to go in. They wore long garments like striped sailor suits. Nora hugged herself. 'I look like a peppermint humbug!' she moaned. 'Let's just run into the sea before anyone sees.'

'Race you!' yelled Erin. She sprinted across the sand and went splashing into the water, shrieking at the cold. Nora followed, ploughing through the surf, squealing as loudly as her sister.

Lizzie ran down to the edge of the whispering white surf, but stopped just before she reached it. Up ahead, the twins were throwing handfuls of water at one another and screaming. Lizzie dipped her toe in and felt the delightful icy touch of the water, sluicing over her feet and washing up to her ankles. She wriggled her feet and felt her toes sinking in a little way. What a peculiar, wonderful feeling. She stared, transfixed, at all the tiny bubbles in the sea foam.

Dru waded in, with Hari close behind, then Malachy who left his crutch lying on the beach. 'Just come in a little way,' Malachy suggested.

'In me clothes?'

'Why not?'

Lizzie sloshed her feet through the water. 'It's too cold.'

'It's easier if you do it all at once. You soon get used to it.'

'I ain't ready yet!' she shouted, annoyed.

'Do I have to come and drag you in like an octopus?' Erin teased. 'It's only the sea, you big eejit. It won't bite you.'

'Leave off,' Malachy told her. 'Let her do it in her own time.'

Dru was already swimming back and forth, his long arms plunging under the waves with total confidence. Lizzie laughed at his huffing, puffing face every time it emerged from the water. He looked like a little mole.

Hari held out his hand, reminding Lizzie of the train and how scared she'd been of that. 'We've come all this way to the sea, so come on in. It's nicer than you think.'

'I don't know how to swim,' she finally admitted, shame-faced. Standing there in her dress, with the waves up to her shins, she felt like a total buffoon. Everyone would laugh at her now, she knew it.

But Hari just smiled. 'I see. Would you let me teach you, then?'

'Could ... could you do that?'

'I can certainly try.'

Hari led her into the deeper water, and she squealed as the cold bit into her legs and body. 'It's ruddy freezing!'

'I learned to swim in the Arabian Sea,' Hari said. 'It was a lot warmer than this.'

While the others looked on and waved encouragingly, Hari patiently talked Lizzie through the basics. The cold water didn't seem so cold once you were moving around, kicking your legs and thrashing about with your arms. He taught her to tread water first, and when she'd got the hang of that, she tried a doggie paddle.

'Swim to me.' Hari waded a little way further out. 'It's only a few feet. You can do this.'

'Right,' Lizzie puffed. 'Just watch me.' Mustering all her willpower, she churned away at the water, kicking and scrabbling with her arms and – to her delight – realized she wasn't sinking. She kept Hari in sight, swimming for all she was worth, and only saw the huge wave rearing up behind him when it was too late.

She shrieked as the wave deluged them both. Salty water filled her mouth and nose. Moments later she stood, coughing and spitting, her hair draggled down all around her. There was something wet and slimy in her face, tangled through her hair.

She picked it out. It was seaweed. Dru was watching her and, expecting him to laugh, she got ready to fling it at him in anger.

But he didn't laugh. 'You look like a mermaid, Lizzie,' he said gallantly.

She turned away. 'Blimey. I'm covered in goose pimples. I'm for drying off.'

* * *

Nobody had any towels, so they lay on the beach in the strong late summer sunshine, chatting quietly and letting the sun dry them. Lizzie couldn't remember ever having felt more at peace. 'I don't want to get up ever again,' she sighed. 'I'll lie here until I starve to death.'

'No need to starve,' Malachy said. 'There's a cockle girl up yonder.'

Dru sat up. '*Formidable!* Cockles and whelks all round, my treat.'

Before Lizzie could stop him, he'd put his fingers in his mouth and blown a shrill whistle, which brought the girl running. She was Lizzie's age, with curly hair as black as Whitby jet and a tray hung around her neck from a leather strap. Her polite smile changed to a more honest grin when she drew close and saw them all together.

'You lot look like trouble,' she joked. 'You'd better have money. If you think I'm giving these away, you can hop off.'

'*Bien sûr!*' Dru said, pretending to be offended.

At the sound of his accent, the girl turned a little pink and giggled. 'Very well, *monsieur*. What'll it be?'

Dru bought some pots of cockles and whelks to share. He added a dash of vinegar to his and tucked in. Lizzie stared at the strange slimy things, wondering if she could eat something so odd-looking, but the cockles turned out to be gorgeous despite looking like something Akula might sneeze up.

The girl stayed to chat. Her name, they soon learned, was Elsie. When she asked innocently if they were servants for a rich family on holiday in Whitby, the Penny Gaff Gang grinned at one another, wondering who should be the one to explain.

'We're with the circus,' Lizzie eventually said.

'Get away!'

To prove it, they showed her the posters and pointed out first Dru, then the twins. Elsie seemed star-struck after that, mumbling shyly, especially at Dru.

Lizzie tried to draw her out again. 'It's lovely here,' she said. 'Beautiful and peaceful. Not like smelly old London. You're so lucky to live here by the sea.'

'You reckon?' Elsie said, giving her an odd look. 'Don't let the sunshine and the seaside tomfoolery trick you. It's a different story after dark.'

Lizzie felt the hairs on her scalp prickle. Maybe now she'd learn why she'd had a vision foretelling her arrival. 'How d'you mean?'

'Whitby's haunted,' Elsie said in a voice barely

above a whisper.

'By who?'

'The ghosts of drowned sailors. Those who've died at sea, like. The fog comes rolling in, and they drift with it, up the beach and into the wet streets. If you're very quiet, you can hear them tap-tap-tappin' on the windows. They want their loved ones to come down and let them in. But you must never do that, or you'll be a cold corpse yourself come the morning.'

Lizzie had fresh goose flesh on her arms. She knew ghosts were real. She'd seen them and spoken to them. Even though the story Elsie was spinning sounded like a fireside tale – the sort of thing children tried to spook one another with – it still reminded her of her vision.

'The sailors come on a ghost ship,' Elsie went on. 'It sails in on a cloud of mist, and from time to time it spirits living souls away, never to be seen again. Some say the captain is the Devil himself.'

Now Lizzie's spine was crawling. *A ghost ship? That's what I saw!*

'That's one of your local legends, is it?' Malachy said.

'It's the gospel truth. I've seen the ghost ship out at sea with my very own eyes.'

Lizzie was about to tell her to stop joshing, but the

fear in the girl's eyes was real. She meant it.

'Where from?' Malachy said, curious now.

'Our cottage up by the harbour,' she told him. 'I saw it through my window, shrouded in mist, flickering with a right queer light. I couldn't sleep for thinking of it!' She stood up suddenly and brushed the sand off her dress. 'Lovely to chat to you all, but I'll take me leave of you now, if you don't mind. Good day.'

After eating their cockles, the children strolled along the harbour. Dru darted off without warning, then came running up to Lizzie five minutes later. 'I bought you a present,' he gasped. 'Some rock.'

Lizzie laughed. 'There's tons of rock all over the place. On the beach, on the cliffs … you didn't need to pay for it.'

'*This* sort of rock, *ma belle*.' He passed her a stick of something wrapped in paper. 'You eat it.'

Lizzie unwrapped it, giving Dru suspicious glances, and took a testing bite. An explosion of minty sweetness went off in her mouth. She rewarded him with a smile of pure delight.

Meanwhile, Nora and Erin were chatting to a man in a straw boater and striped jacket. He was tanned and handsome, and Lizzie thought that he looked Italian or even Greek. He stood behind a table draped with a blue cloth, with three shells set out on it.

'Oh, I know this grift,' Lizzie told Dru. 'One of Pa's mates used to do it. We need to warn 'em. He tricks you into thinking you know which shell the pea's under.'

'I think Erin knows exactly what she's doing,' Dru said.

'Now, my name's Billy,' the man said. 'What might your name be, sweetheart?'

'It might be Queen Titania,' said Erin, hands on hips. 'But it's not.'

'Now those lips have kissed the Blarney stone, or I'm a monkey's uncle!' laughed Billy. 'First time in my life I've ever been jealous of a lump of masonry.' He rubbed his hands together. 'Now you've clearly got the gift of the gab, my sweet colleen, but do you have the luck of the Irish along with it? I've got a shiny shilling here for you if you do. What's the catch, you ask? It's a penny in. That's all. Who wouldn't risk a penny to win a shilling, eh?'

'Listen to him talk!' Lizzie whispered.

Erin slapped a penny down on the table and Billy started back with mock surprise. 'Steady on, my duck, no need to start wrecking the place! Now, this is a game we call Find the Lady.' He held up a dried pea, then put it down and clapped a shell over it, quickly nudging the other shells alongside. 'First go, this one's just for fun, not playing for money yet, keep your eyes on the prize…' His hands moved in a blur, swivelling the shells around one another in figure-eights and quick swaps. 'Which one's it under?'

'That one!' Erin tapped the middle shell.

Billy lifted it, revealing the pea. 'Oh dear,' he said. 'Oh, Mother, I feel faint. I'm done for. She'll make a beggar of me. Ma always said the pretty girls would be my ruin. Another go? For the money this time?'

Erin laughed. 'Why not.'

But this time, to nobody's surprise, the pea wasn't where she'd thought it was. Erin stared in disbelief as Billy unveiled it, winked, and tucked her penny into his waistcoat pocket. 'Any time you want another go-round, my darling, just you come and find me.'

'Where can I find you, then?' Erin said, cocking her head. Lizzie was startled to see her acting so bold and grown-up all of a sudden.

'Walking to and fro upon the earth, and walking up and down on it.' Billy tipped his hat.

Erin strolled back to join them, smiling and

shaking her head.

'You're in a good mood for someone who's just lost money,' Malachy challenged her.

'Ah, it was money well spent,' said Erin. 'He's an entertainer, just like us. Did you hear that patter of his? He's a master at it.'

'Good hands too,' agreed Nora. 'Fast.'

'We should talk to Fitzy. Maybe he'll take Billy on,' Erin suggested. 'We could use a showman like him.'

'Not a chance,' Malachy said. He sounded angry. 'My dad doesn't hire shysters and conmen. Billy can stay down here where he belongs.'

'Come on, Nora,' Erin said. 'Let's walk on a bit.'

As they strolled off, chatting casually and giggling, Malachy glared after them.

Lizzie nudged Dru. 'She was flirtin' with him, wasn't she?' she whispered. 'If her ma knew, she'd skin her alive!'

'So don't tell her,' Dru said, and laughed softly.

CHAPTER 5

The next day, a small crowd was gathered in the vast castle kitchens.

'Mrs Cobbett isn't going to like it, sir,' Johnson told the Maharaja.

'My dear man, Mrs Cobbett is being given the whole afternoon and evening off, as are the rest of the kitchen staff. She has nothing to complain about.'

'But that's her kitchen. She won't want strangers in it.'

'I can hardly ask Mrs Sullivan to cater a picnic dinner for the whole of her circus cast and crew in her little tent, can I?' The Maharaja ushered Johnson out of the castle kitchens, past where Lizzie and the Sullivans stood waiting in the hallway. Johnson glowered at them as he passed.

Ma Sullivan took a deep breath. 'Right, girls! Let's get to work.' She strode into the kitchens and looked around approvingly at the hanging pots and pans, the slate work surfaces, the colossal table and the stove. All the walls were covered with cream-coloured tiles with embossed patterns on. 'Saints preserve us, would you look at the size of this place. I could feed the five thousand with a kitchen like this.'

'Why does the Maharaja think you couldn't cope in your tea tent?' Erin said, casting a wary eye over the dangling ladles and knives. 'You feed us all every day with your dear little stove.'

'Ah, but not all at once, cushla, and that's the point.' Ma Sullivan rolled up her sleeves. 'The Maharaja wants a grand feast, and a grand feast he shall have.'

Flora, the circus's Fat Lady, fat as a Christmas pudding, and the Amazon Queen, tall and mahogany-brown, let themselves into the kitchen. 'Heard it was all hands to the pump,' Flora said. 'What can we do to 'elp?'

'You heard right. I'll need spuds peeled, chickens

plucked, apples cored, and anything this lot don't have in their stores we'll have to send to town for.'

So that afternoon it was Ma Sullivan who was the ringmaster, taking over the castle kitchens and ransacking the stores, while Nora, Erin and Lizzie scurried around doing whatever they were told and trying not to get under anybody's feet. Lizzie did her best, but she wasn't used to cooking, and when she tried to chop an onion it shot across the room like a cannonball. Taking the knife off her, Ma Sullivan sent Lizzie off on an errand instead.

'We'll need ice for the ice cream. You know where it's kept?'

'The ice house?'

'Clever girl.'

Lizzie had seen the ice house earlier, a gloomy stone building like a tiny tomb, cold enough to store ice in the summer. As she crossed the lawn, she saw the castle staff setting up tables and chairs and laying delicate white cloths out. *It's going to be a proper fancy dinner party*, she thought, and felt a surge of excitement. Tonight she'd dine with royalty. It was a long way from the squalor and hunger of Rat's Castle where she'd started out.

Johnson was shepherding the rest of the staff about, grumpily ordering them to set a table down here or a chair there, and to mind the ruddy flowerbeds while they did it. As Lizzie watched, the Maharaja came strolling over in his shooting coat, smoking a fat cigar and nodding in approval.

'Capital work, Johnson,' he said.

'With respect, sir, you oughtn't to be hosting this party at all.'

'Why on earth not?'

'I'd be wary of showing off your wealth in front of all these strangers. I wouldn't let them into my home, neither. They don't have much, by the look of them, and envy can make people light-fingered.'

Gurinder Bhatti waved away the comment. 'They are my guests. Now, you have your instructions, Mister Johnson. I expect you to carry them out. Good man.' He walked away, whistling to himself.

Johnson stared after him. He was turning beetroot-coloured with anger again. 'Marching about like he owns the bloomin' place, when he's only the tenant,' he muttered. 'He'll learn. Oh, he'll learn. "From him who hath much, much shall be taken away."'

Lizzie found Hari down by the ice house. Her friend

was poking around in the gravel, and jumped when he saw Lizzie.

'What you up to?' she asked him.

'Just examining the local rocks,' Hari said casually. 'You can find lots of interesting fossils here on the coast.'

'Right,' Lizzie said, eyeing him curiously. 'What's so interesting about them?'

'They're the remains of ancient animals,' Hari explained.

'Well, sorry to drag you away from your old animal rocks, but can you help me carry some ice?' Lizzie asked.

They each gathered up a block of ice from the dark straw-packed cavity inside the building. 'We should drop some of this down old Johnson's back,' Lizzie giggled. 'Help him cool off.'

'Is he shouting about his lawns again?'

'He's angry at the Maharaja for telling him what to do. I dunno why. He's a servant, ain't he? He gets paid to do what he's told.'

'Some white people think brown people are meant to take orders, not give them. If someone with dark skin tells them what to do, it turns their whole world upside down.'

'Gawd. I never even thought of that.'

Hari shrugged. 'Why would you? You're white.'

'It must be hard for you and your uncle, looking different.'

'Different,' Hari said thoughtfully. 'Do you know what they call brown-skinned people in India?'

'No, what?'

'People.'

Later that afternoon, Ma Sullivan was in despair.

'Lizzie, Lord love you, do you even know one end of a knife from another? I asked you to top and tail those green beans, and you've murdered them in cold blood!'

Lizzie, who had held the kitchen knife with both hands and hacked at the beans like a maniac until green fragments flew across the room, was not discouraged. 'I can still help. Just give me something else to do.'

'Can you beat an egg white until it's stiff?'

'Dunno,' Lizzie said brightly. 'Never tried.'

Ma Sullivan heaved a sigh that seemed to come from the pit of her stomach. 'Best not, then. I'm scared to think what might come of it. Tell you what, let's set you to buttering the bread. Saints help us if you can't manage that.'

''Course I can butter a slice of bread!' Lizzie scoffed.

Ma Sullivan set her to work, and asked in a softer voice, 'Did you never help with the cooking at home, love?'

Lizzie shrugged. 'There weren't ever much to cook, even when my ma was alive. Pa took all the money and spent it on drink.'

'Mother of mercy,' Ma Sullivan said, shaking her head. 'No wonder you were all skin and bones when you joined up with Fitzy's.' She whipped up egg whites and sugar into a foamy froth, then blobbed them out on a baking tray.

Nora and Erin looked on excitedly. 'Are you making meringues, Ma?'

'I surely am. We'll have whipped cream and cherries, and we can use some of that ice to do a blackberry sorbet.'

Lizzie's mouth watered at the thought of a table laden with desserts. 'How'd you know how to make all this posh nosh?' she asked. 'Cakes is one thing, but this is a bit classy, innit?'

'I used to be in service!' Ma Sullivan said proudly. Her kindly eyes crinkled with amusement. 'Picture me in a pinafore, if you will.'

'Our ma worked in a big house like this one, so she did,' Erin butted in. 'The lord of the manor took a fancy to her, and she was only eighteen, and it was right scandalous.'

'That he did, and that it was, and I was having none of it, so I ran away – Nora, would you check the red cabbage, it's boiling dry for heaven's sake. I met my dear Mister Sullivan in a ballroom in Galway. Before you could whistle, I'd run off to join the circus!' She laughed loudly over the sound of bubbling pots and rattling lids.

Lizzie loved hearing Ma Sullivan's stories, when the twins would let her finish them. 'Fitzy must have been a young man then.'

'No, this wasn't Fitzy's. We joined up with a fella name of Lovett. American, he was. Used to tour with a Wild West show, like Sean and the boys do now. We travelled with him for a while – Flora, see if the pantry's got a spare bottle of sherry for the trifle, and sure I'll have one myself while you're at it! – then with a load of other circuses until we threw in with Fitzy a few years ago.'

'Do you ever miss it? Being in service?'

'Miss it? *Miss it?*' Ma Sullivan laughed until Lizzie worried she might hurt herself. 'Oh, Lizzie, you do say the silliest things. Miss being bossed around by a bunch of toffs who look down on you all the time? Who could miss that?' She paused and looked around. 'Ah, but a grand kitchen like this, it's wasted on the likes of Mrs Cobbett. I could work wonders in this place.'

Months ago, when Dru had been arrested by the London police in the belief he was the mysterious Phantom burglar, Lizzie had brought the real villain to light and saved Dru's life. His sister Collette, who had been icy and harsh with Lizzie before, changed her attitude overnight. Her gratitude and affection were a bit embarrassing.

Still, she did know fashion, and had given Lizzie a stunning dress she'd outgrown. It was meant to be 'for best', but was so beautiful that Lizzie had never worn it. She sometimes unfolded it, just to look at, and then put it away again. Silly. When would she ever get a chance to dress up in fancy clothes while she was living this circus life, constantly on the road?

'It's time,' she whispered, unfolding the parcel of crackly brown paper. A waft of lavender went up; Collette had left some in the dress's folds to protect against moths.

The dress was blue silk, with a black lace overlay and beaded buttons. Lizzie changed into it, looked at herself in the mirror and made a little excited noise in her throat. She wasn't sure how she could eat, with these butterflies in her stomach.

On impulse, she snatched up her mother's tortoiseshell comb and arranged it in her brown hair, just so. Perfect. 'Time to go and meet the quality,' she told her reflection. 'Wish you could be here too, Ma.'

The sun was setting behind the turrets of Dunsley Castle. All the circus folk were gathered on the lawn, dressed in their finest clothes. Lizzie stared at the clowns, unrecognizable in evening dress. She could tell that some last-minute sewing jobs had been carried out, and some collars had been freshened up with chalk, but at least they had made the effort.

She, Nora and Erin slowly walked over to where Dru, Hari and Malachy were standing below a tree.

Nora and Erin were in identical dresses of rust-coloured silk, their hair patiently combed through and tied up in bows. The boys all looked like young men in their evening dress. A strange silence fell as they looked one another up and down.

Malachy coughed. 'Erin, you look, um…'

She cocked her head. 'Cat got your tongue?'

'You're all so…' Hari couldn't get the words out. Nora raised an eyebrow and smirked.

Dru came to their rescue. 'Ladies, you are all exquisite. It would be our honour if you would accompany us to the table. Gentlemen, *allons-y*.'

He offered Lizzie his arm and she took it, her heart thumping. She felt ever so grown-up all of a sudden, carrying on like this.

The Maharaja spread his hands in welcome. He wore his full ceremonial ensemble, from the turban festooned with pearls to the great lengths of rich crimson silk that draped his arms and waist. But it was the woman behind him who drew everyone's attention.

'My friend, the Lady Susannah de Montefiore,' he said proudly. It was the same blonde woman he'd been sitting with at the Oxford performance, but now she was dressed in deep indigo and wore so much black jet jewellery that it put the window display at Delingpole's to shame.

Everybody stood in a line, ready to be introduced to the pair, and a hubbub of whispered conversation began.

'She's so beautiful,' Lizzie whispered to the Sullivans.

Mrs Sullivan sucked at her cheeks. 'Aye, she's a looker, and don't she know it?'

'Ma!' said Nora through clenched teeth.

'I speak as I find,' Ma Sullivan said firmly. 'She's a little too full of herself for my liking.' She narrowed her eyes. 'She reminds me of someone too. Was it ... no, can't place her. Probably one of the posh people I used to work for. Lord knows there were enough of those.'

Fitzy worked his way down the line, introducing the Maharaja to each member of the circus in turn. The Maharaja shook their hands enthusiastically and seemed every bit as excited as he had been in the show tent. He was full of questions: did Mario the Mighty have a special diet? Was every clown's make-up truly unique? How old was Leo the lion?

He was especially excited to meet Lizzie. 'The famous fortune-teller! I tried palm-reading myself, you know, but I never had the knack for it. Do you do séances? I've been to a few in London, where a psychic communicated with spirits.'

Lady Susannah, who had been quiet until now, spoke up before Lizzie could answer. 'You're a clairvoyant?'

'Yes, ma'am,' Lizzie said, giving a little curtsey. Was that the right thing to do? She had absolutely no idea.

'I'm sure you're very convincing,' the lady said, with a gracious smile. She turned to the Maharaja. 'It's all an act, my love. They work it all out with special signals and so forth. She doesn't really have mysterious powers.'

'She does,' Hari insisted. 'You should let her do a reading for you. You won't doubt her after that, I promise you.'

'Well,' Lady Susannah said with a light laugh, 'perhaps that can be arranged.'

'I love your jewellery!' Nora burst out, unable to contain herself. 'It's just beautiful.'

Erin glared at her sister, but Lady Susannah didn't seem to mind. 'Jet is popular in London too,' she smiled. 'For the same reason as séances are, I am sorry to say. Grief for the dead. Our beloved Queen Victoria is wearing it in mourning.'

The Maharaja sighed. 'Indeed. Poor, dear Victoria. Since her husband Albert passed away, she is quite inconsolable. I fear she will waste away altogether from sheer grief.'

It gave Lizzie a giddy feeling to think that the man standing before her was a close friend of the Queen of England. 'Poor thing,' she said, not knowing what else to say.

'Don't tell the Queen,' said the Maharaja with a wink, 'but I have a gift I think will bring fire back into her heart again. Mum's the word, eh?'

Lizzie suddenly had a hunch. The word *sparkling* had popped into her mind. 'Is it jet jewellery?' she guessed.

'Oh, no!' the Maharaja laughed, lifting a chubby finger. 'My present is far more valuable than jet.'

Lizzie noticed Lady Susannah giving him a somewhat frosty look, but said nothing. *Is the lady jealous of Queen Victoria?* she wondered. It must be a truly amazing present…

The Maharaja moved on down the line. Nora sighed and muttered, 'Look at all that jet. It's lying on her in heaps! Oh, I'd do anything for some of my own!'

'You don't need jewellery,' Hari said in a shy voice. 'You're pretty enough as you are.'

'I thought you only fancied fossils?' Lizzie teased.

Nora hadn't heard properly, and spun around

indignantly. 'Did you just call me a *fossil*, Hari?'

* * *

Later on, as they were about to sit down to dinner, Lizzie glanced out over the castle grounds. Dusk was setting in, but the sea was still dimly visible in the far distance. Just as she was fondly remembering how it felt to swim there, a strange greenish light appeared, flickering across the waves. It was only there for a second, then it was gone.

She rubbed her eyes and looked again. *Probably just my imagination*, she thought. It's been a long, busy day…

The light flickered again. Was she seeing things, or was it coming from a misty cloud on the sea?

A chill ran through her. She'd seen that sight in her vision; now she was seeing it in real life. She remembered what Elsie the cockle girl had said about the ghosts of drowned sailors returning to the town after dark. The light she was seeing now must be the same light Elsie had spoken fearfully about…

The light of the ghost ship.

CHAPTER 6

Lizzie woke up in her caravan still feeling full. So, it hadn't been a dream – she really had gorged herself on roast chicken, mashed potato, gravy and tiny sweet peas, and then plate after plate of meringues drowning in thick cream, and cherries as crimson as the Maharaja's ruby rings.

She sat up, noticing that her limbs still ached a little. Ah, yes. The dancing. The Maharaja had clapped his hands, the band had begun to play, and everyone had begun to dance in couples and singles across the lawns, around the tents and in and out of the bushes, laughing as they went. Erin and Malachy, Hari and Nora, and Dru with her…

'Phew.' She fell back against her mound of pillows. 'It's a good job I ain't a princess. I don't reckon I've got the puff for it.'

Her memories of the night before were a bit hazy, but she remembered still being up at past one in the morning. No wonder she felt exhausted. *Tea*, she thought. *What I need is a nice hot cup of tea.*

She quickly dressed and headed over to Ma Sullivan's catering tent. To her surprise, it was empty, with only Ma Sullivan herself waiting behind the counter. 'She's alive!' Ma Sullivan laughed. 'Saints be praised.'

'Where is everybody? What time is it?'

'It'll be about eight o'clock, my dear. Everybody's already up and rehearsing. Tea and toast, is it?'

'Just tea, thanks. I don't think I'll need to eat again for about a week.'

Lizzie took a seat, and soon Ma Sullivan brought tea over for them both. 'I'm not in trouble, am I?' Lizzie asked. 'For sleeping in?'

'Bless you, no. You're not in the show. It's only the performers who are at work already. They want to make this show really special for the Maharaja, you see. He's already seen the regular routine in Oxford, so they're trying to work out some new stunts.'

'Oh. I'm at a bit of a loose end today, then. I know! I could help you make a birthday cake for Erin and Nora!'

'That's sweet of you, Liz, but it's all under control. I wouldn't want to put you to the trouble.' Ma smiled in a sly way. 'Now if I was in your shoes, I'd be finishing what I started last night.'

Lizzie gawped. 'Finishing what?'

'Oh, don't make out like you don't know. I saw you and Dru dancing the night away, out under the stars.'

'So? All we did was have a dance!' Lizzie exclaimed. 'You're a rotten old tease, you are.'

'You think I don't remember what it's like to be young?' Ma Sullivan winked.

'We're just friends. Can't friends have a dance together?'

Ma Sullivan laughed like a horse. 'There's none so blind as those that will not see! Go on, be off with you. Go make yourself useful in the show tent.'

Lizzie finished her tea before she left. It gave her a hearty warm feeling inside, just like Ma Sullivan's laughter did.

She slipped into the show tent unseen. Rehearsals

were underway, each group in their own area. The clowns had one corner, the acrobats another, and up above on the high wire, Dru and Collette were polishing their routine.

She quietly took a seat at the back. Dru went promenading up and down the tightrope in a bathing costume, carrying his sister on his shoulders. She carried a parasol, which she twirled like a giant wheel, catching the light. By the look of it, they had revamped their act to give it a seaside theme. *That should give the locals a smile*, Lizzie thought.

Dru paused in the middle of the tightrope. His father Pierre, sporting a fine black moustache curled up at the ends, threw him a stick of rock, followed rapidly by two more. Dru juggled the rock sticks, wobbling back and forth, while Collette snatched at them, never quite managing to get one.

I know what gave you that idea, Lizzie thought happily.

'Excuse me? Everyone? May I please have your attention?' It was the Maharaja, wringing his hands and standing in the entrance to the tent. 'Something terrible has happened.'

As the circus folk saw the distraught look on his

face, they stopped what they were doing and turned to listen. Dru deftly caught all three rock sticks in the same hand and hurried to the end of the wire, where he set Collette down with infinite care.

Lizzie could feel a hard egg of fear growing in her throat. The Maharaja looked dark-eyed and sick. His shirt was hanging out. *Someone's been murdered,* she thought. *Or found dead in their bed, a cold corpse in the morning. That light I saw last night ... Elsie tried to warn us about ghosts coming up from the harbour.* She told herself not to get carried away. Whatever might be going on, she should listen and help. That was what her powers were for, wasn't it?

'There's been a b-b-burglary,' the Maharaja stammered. 'Last night, while Lady Susannah was asleep in her bedchamber, her jet jewellery was stolen.'

Everyone looked at each other uneasily. There were a few murmurs and gasps and some of the circus people looked weary and miserable, as if they'd known this was all too good to last. Lizzie felt that way too. It had all been going too well. Even though Johnson was wary of them, they'd been made welcome here. And now this...

'I have to ask,' the Maharaja went on, 'if anyone

here saw anything suspicious after the dinner party. Anything at all.'

Here we go again, Lizzie thought with a heavy heart. Even though she'd only been in the circus a short while, she had quickly learned that many people had a low opinion of circus folk. Most assumed they were all criminals. She'd never forget the London policemen who had treated her like a thief on sight.

One of the clowns, Didi, spoke with a voice shaking with anger. 'If we'd seen anything suspicious, sir, I expect we'd have said so at the time.' He looked around. 'I think I speak for all of us.'

The Maharaja realized what Didi was upset about. 'My dear man, I don't mean any offence. I am quite sure nobody here is involved in this dreadful deed. I am simply asking for your help in catching the culprit.'

That took the wind out of Didi's sails. 'Ah. Well, I do beg your pardon. We'll all keep our eyes open, won't we, fellas?'

A chorus of 'yes!' and 'of course!' was his answer.

'I am in your debt, my friends,' the Maharaja said. 'Any detail you might recall, however insignificant it might seem, could be of help. They told me Whitby was cursed, but I laughed in their faces. How I wish I had not. My poor Lady Susannah is quite beside herself with grief.'

I bet she is, Lizzie thought. The lady had been so proud of her jewels. Maybe whoever had taken them had been jealous of her wealth, or wanted to humble her. Someone from her past perhaps?

As the Maharaja turned to leave, she stood up and called 'Wait!' at the top of her voice. She ran from her seat down to the startled man.

'Yes? You saw something, my dear?'

'No,' she gasped, 'but I might.'

The Maharaja looked blank.

'I could read her palm,' Lizzie explained. 'I see things. I might have a vision of what really happened. Who it was that done it.'

The Maharaja didn't seem to know what to say to that. 'Thank you,' he eventually said, with great respect. 'I will pass on your kind offer to Lady Susannah. She is far too upset right now, but when she calms down, perhaps you could offer to do … whatever it is you do.'

Once the Maharaja had gone, Hari went and sat next to Lizzie. 'You're really going to help him?'

'Of course. Why wouldn't I?'

'I always thought your powers were meant to be

used for good,' Hari said. There was a coldness in his voice that Lizzie didn't like.

'I feel sorry for him, and for her. It ain't nice to have your stuff stolen, is it?'

Hari laughed bitterly. 'Have you ever heard of *karma*, Lizzie?'

'Can't say I have.'

'There's a saying you English have that sums it up pretty well: "What goes around, comes around." I'm not going to be crying any tears for the Maharaja having his jewels stolen. Not when he's stolen jewels from his people in India!'

''Scuse me,' Lizzie said, confused at his attitude. 'I'm ... I'm going for a walk.' She strode off, feeling like everything was turning sour all of a sudden. Maybe the circus would have been better off in Reading after all.

The tables and chairs were still set out from the previous night's party, though they were bare now. Nora was sitting there alone, her arms flat on the table top, her head resting on the backs of her hands. Lizzie thought she was asleep until she saw her friend's eyes were open. She was gazing up at the castle.

'What you up to?'

'Wondering which one is her window,' Nora sighed.

Lizzie sat down next to her. 'I hate this. It was supposed to be so much fun. The Maharaja's just tryin' to cheer everyone up, and now this happens!'

'Poor Lady Susannah,' said Nora. 'That jewellery was gorgeous.'

'Jet costs a packet,' Lizzie agreed, remembering Delingpole's.

'I know,' Nora sighed. 'But it's not just that, is it? It was a gift from him. From her handsome prince.'

'I didn't even think of that.' *Nora is surprisingly romantic sometimes*, Lizzie thought. Her friend dreamed of castles and fairy-tale weddings. She was so different from Erin, who made rude jokes and flirted with cheeky conmen on the sea front. Although the twins looked identical, their personalities were complete opposites.

'So who'd you think did it?' Nora asked. 'You must have had a vision, or something. You're always getting them over stuff like this.'

'I haven't a clue!' Lizzie said, shaking her head. 'No visions, no dreams, not a dicky bird.'

Nora frowned in thought. 'It must have been someone who could have got inside the castle,' she announced, like a detective making a clever deduction.

'Well, that could have been anyone!' Lizzie scoffed.

86

'There's no security here to speak of, is there?'

'Suppose not.'

'The Maharaja's like a great big cuddly sheepdog. He thinks everyone's his friend. He's just too trusting.'

Nora's lip trembled. 'Why did this have to happen, Lizzie? Why can't things just be … just be *nice*?'

Lizzie put a comforting arm around her friend's shoulder. But the second her body touched Nora's, a vision exploded into her mind, sudden and forceful as a blow to the face. She whimpered and clutched her forehead, her fingers jerking as if trying to rip the unwanted vision out of her mind and fling it away.

'Lizzie?' Nora gasped. She pulled away. 'What can you see?'

'I…'

She couldn't tell her. The vision was still there, fixed in her mind like a nightmare that doesn't fade even after waking.

In her mind's eye, she saw Nora. She was holding her long hair out of the way and fastening a stunning necklace round her neck. It was made from rich, black jet.

'Are you all right? Do you want a drink of water?'

'Would you?' Lizzie croaked. 'I'll wait here. Thanks.'

As Nora ran off, Lizzie sat feeling sick to her stomach.

She didn't really want a drink – she just had to make Nora go away, at least until that horrible vision was out of her head.

You know what it means, a nasty voice whispered at the back of her mind.

'I don't believe it,' Lizzie muttered to herself.

But an idea was taking shape in her imagination, even though she hated it. Nora had pined after that jet necklace like a lovesick schoolgirl. She'd gazed into the window at Delingpole's, talking about how much she wanted jet jewellery of her own.

Could she have stolen it?

Lizzie thought back to how Nora had been only minutes before. Had she been staring at the window out of guilt? When she asked Lizzie if she'd had a vision, had there been a touch of panic in her voice – as if she feared to be found out?

'Stop it!' she yelled to herself. She smacked herself on the side of the head, hard enough to hurt. That brought her to her senses. Mercifully, the vision began to fade and Lizzie felt dreadful now. Nora had become like a sister to her. She'd never had a best friend before. Nora was utterly loyal, kind-hearted and trusting. She'd *never* steal, no matter how much she coveted something that belonged to someone else.

'Feeling any better?' Nora said. She passed Lizzie her glass of water.

'Much,' said Lizzie, forcing a smile.

But a cold worm of worry was still coiling and looping deep down in her stomach. No matter how much she might trust Nora, she knew her visions had never been wrong before. Even Malachy had admitted it. She looked up into her friend's troubled, concerned face, and wished she could say what was in her heart.

CHAPTER 7

Later that day, as the Penny Gaff Gang gathered in the gardens before their second trip into Whitby, Hari was reluctant to go.

'Come on, Hari, stretch your legs! It'll be fun!' Erin tugged at Hari's arm. Lizzie wondered if she meant to drag him all the way to Whitby.

'I can't,' Hari said. 'I told you, I've got chores to do.'

'But we're at the seaside!'

'You could always help me clean out the lion cage if you want. My uncle will gladly give you a shovel.'

Erin sighed and let him go. 'I don't know what's gotten into you lot. Yesterday you couldn't wait to get down to Whitby. Today you're like a load of old ladies.'

'Everyone's just worn out after rehearsal and last night, probably,' Lizzie said. 'The sea air'll soon freshen us up.'

'It's not the sea air that Erin's looking forward to,' Nora grinned, giving Lizzie a nudge. Lizzie smiled back, sharing the joke, but still felt awkward around Nora, and felt horrible for feeling awkward.

As the Penny Gaff Gang headed towards the coast road and Whitby, Lizzie looked out towards the sea and wondered what secrets were hiding out there. How could such a bright, sunlit place be so creepy and mysterious after dark? Looking at the sea now, legends of ghost ships and supernatural mists seemed daft.

But she'd seen that green light last night, and the fog bank. Whether they were the work of ghosts or not, they were real. Lizzie struggled to think of another explanation. An ordinary ship might shine a light, but a *green* one?

Maybe she should ask the Maharaja if she could watch from one of the castle's towers and get a better view. She looked over her shoulder back towards Dunsley Castle, and to her surprise saw a dark-skinned figure hurrying away from the grounds.

Whoever it was, he was heading for the moors.

She squinted. Was that Hari? Why would Hari lie about needing to stay behind at the circus? Lizzie puzzled over that for a while. Perhaps he just needed to spend some time alone. After all, there wasn't much privacy to be had when you were part of a circus. Hari didn't have his own trailer like Lizzie did.

Besides, she thought, as she saw Johnson the gardener digging in his flowerbeds, there were plenty of people here that Hari probably wanted to stay away from.

Johnson raised his ugly head as they approached. 'Mind you stay away from these rosebeds!' he shouted. 'Prize-winners, they are. Not that the likes of you would care.'

'We're not going anywhere near your flowers!' Lizzie shouted back angrily. It was true, obviously so. They weren't even heading in that direction.

Erin stuck out her jaw and gave Johnson a poisonous glare. Lizzie thought she might go and jump right in the middle of the flowerbeds, just to give old Johnson a heart attack. But Erin respected Fitzy, and Fitzy had promised they'd respect the gardens.

'We're going to the harbour,' Erin said, turning

her back on him.

'Is that so?' Johnson snarled. 'You'd best be back before dark. Else you might be spirited away like the others before you.'

Lizzie felt Malachy's arm leading her off. 'Just walk away,' he said quietly. 'It's the best thing to do, always.'

Lizzie went with him. 'Sorry, Mal. These threats … it just makes me so angry.'

Everywhere the circus went, they met distrust and suspicion. Lizzie hated it. Nobody in her life had been kinder to her than the people of Fitzy's Circus. Nobody deserved this treatment less than they did.

Lizzie stayed in a black mood for the duration of the walk to Whitby. The sun, close to noon, was fierce and had no clouds to give any relief. The road, which must have been muddy not long ago, was baked to a dusty crisp.

She lagged behind the others and kicked loose stones off into the shrubbery. If it hadn't been for the lure of the sea, she'd have turned around and gone back to tell Johnson exactly what she thought of him. But she did want to swim again, even if it meant wading in in her clothes like yesterday. She'd never need to be afraid of the water again if only she could learn how to swim.

The welcome sight of the sea shimmering in the distance blew Lizzie's bad mood away like so much smoke. She couldn't stay in a sulk with all that beautiful water out there. Already it seemed less threatening than it had before.

'Hari is not here,' Dru said, noticing her smile. 'Perhaps you will let me be your swimming teacher today?'

'I think I'll be fine on my own,' Lizzie said, feeling awkward. After their dance on the lawn, a swimming lesson would just be too much. Besides, she didn't want him to help her. She'd show him what a fast learner she was.

Soon they were hurrying down the zigzag steps and onto the beach. A lovely great stripe of glistening sand lay before them, unspoiled by footprints. Gulls strutted back and forth on the cliff above, waiting for some dropped morsel.

Lizzie took her shoes and socks off, wishing she had a proper bathing suit and wondering how much they cost. The sand squished beneath her feet delightfully.

She was glad to see fewer people were here this time. They had this whole stretch of beach to themselves.

Well, almost. Someone was sitting on a wooden breakwater with his back to them, his arm around a young blonde woman. Lizzie recognized his stripy jacket at once.

'Isn't that Billy? That bloke who did the pea and shell game?'

'It is too!' Malachy said, with a mixed chuckle and snort.

'Doesn't look like him to me.' Erin sniffed and turned away. 'Are we going swimming or aren't we?'

But Lizzie was still watching. Billy – it was definitely him – turned to give the blonde woman a kiss. Lizzie gasped and ran to Erin's side. 'He's got a girl. Billy's kissing someone! Here, Erin, your beau's been snapped up.'

Erin shrugged, pretending not to care. 'So? He was too old for me anyway.'

'Of course he was,' Malachy said, suddenly sounding more cheerful. 'Good job you didn't talk my dad into taking him on. Imagine if you had.'

'You sure you're OK?' Nora asked her sister. She touched her arm, but Erin swatted it away.

'I said I was fine!' she said a little snappily.

'Never mind, Erin,' Lizzie said. With a wicked grin, she bent over and scooped up a starfish that was lying in a rock pool at her feet. 'There's plenty more fish in the sea!'

She threw the starfish to Erin, who caught it without realizing what it was. As it wriggled in her hands, she let out a shriek and dropped it. 'Oh, you little *devil*! I'll flatten you!'

'Got to catch me first,' Lizzie laughed. She raced into the sea, knowing full well that Erin wouldn't follow her until she'd changed into her bathing costume. Lizzie stood with the sea foaming around her shins, sticking her tongue out, while Erin fumed and flapped and finally started laughing too.

Billy and his girl had quietly slipped away. *Good*, Lizzie thought. *I don't care what Erin says. She doesn't need to see you two canoodling in front of her.*

She felt a little odd, though, standing in the sea all by herself, so she wandered up and down the beach while Erin and Nora changed into their bathing costumes.

A gleam caught her eye. She bent down and saw it was half an oyster shell, rough on one side but pearly and smooth on the other. *It might not be jet*, she thought, *but it's pretty*. If you cut and shaped the pearly bit, it could make a lovely bracelet – the sort of thing a mermaid might wear.

Encouraged, she hunted for more shells and found the beach was rich with them. Her pockets were soon bulging with shells, not just from oysters but scallops and periwinkles too. There'd be enough for matching bracelets for both Erin and Nora.

'What are you up to?' Nora was suddenly by her side, along with the rest of the gang.

Lizzie stood up straight. 'Just beachcombing,' she said secretively.

'Coming for a swim?' Nora duck-dived, her feet kicking up behind her, and swam under the surface. Lizzie watched her bob up again, further out to sea, gasping and triumphant. 'It's lovely once you're under!' she called.

'Right, then,' Lizzie muttered to herself. 'I did it yesterday, I can do it today.' She sloshed away from the shore, gradually submerging herself. Malachy and Dru waved and cheered, egging her on.

Lizzie was up to her neck now. She took a deep breath and ducked her whole head under, thinking, *If I do it on purpose, it won't be so bad*. Everything sounded funny underwater. All she could hear were sloshes and gurgles. Quickly, before she panicked, she burst up to the surface again.

'You're getting the hang of this,' Malachy said, clearly impressed. 'Wish Hari was here to see it.'

Dru did a lazy backstroke for a few yards. 'She was swimming yesterday,' he called. 'Not just wading. Perhaps today, she does not feel up to it.'

His teasing spurred Lizzie on. She lifted her feet from the sea bed and dog-paddled for all she was worth, swimming past the group of her friends and close to where Dru was splashing. She wondered if he was impressed, but she couldn't tell. All her effort went into propelling herself forward.

The water below her swirled and rushed past, pulling her further out to sea. *I can handle this*, she thought. *I'm properly swimming. If only Hari could see me now!*

There were no other swimmers in sight now, and the only thing Lizzie could see out this far were boats. She decided it was time to stop. The undertow had pulled her out a lot farther than she'd meant to come. She put her feet down, expecting to find the sandy sea bed. Her feet went down … and down. As if she'd missed a step going downstairs, they plunged into nothing.

I've gone too far out, she thought in sudden terror. *The water's deep here.* She floundered, gasping, only just managing to keep her head above water. *Remember what Hari showed you*, she thought. *Tread the water, circle your arms, try not to panic.*

But right then a bright crescent of pain split her head in two as if an axe had struck her. Not a cramp but a vision, forcing itself behind her eyes at the worst possible time.

'No!' she gasped as she tried to shut it out. But there was no fighting the vision. It overwhelmed her mind, an image like a macabre illustration from a book of ghost stories.

It was a ship of some kind, with a single mast, looming out of a thick white mist. A sickly green light blazed from the prow, casting eerie shadows across the dark waves. Dimly visible through the mist was a figure – the pilot of this strange vessel.

Lizzie didn't want to look, but her mind's eye swept closer anyway. The figure was wearing a ragged robe, like a hooded spectre from a stage play. It raised its arms, and from the depths of its black hood Lizzie saw two gleaming lights like eyes.

It was real. A ghost ship, captained by Death himself.

Lizzie opened her mouth to scream, and the ocean flooded in. Salt water choked her. Struggling, her strength fading with every second, she sank beneath the water's surface.

The shadow on the ghost ship, still visible in her mind, reached its tattered arms out to grasp her…

CHAPTER 8

Images flashed before Lizzie's eyes. *So*, she thought distantly, *it's true what they say about drowning. You really do see your whole life unfolding in front of you.*

She saw her brother sitting up in bed, coughing blood into a handkerchief. Other memories followed, blindingly fast: her mother hugging her from behind when she was only three, her father roaring drunk and smacking her hard in the face, the Penny Gaff Gang gathered in the tea tent and laughing together.

'Lizzie!'

The voice calling her name seemed to come from far away, a place of dancing light and blue skies. Lizzie thought it might be her mother, calling her to join her in Heaven. Blurry white shapes soared past above her head, above the waves. Were they angels? Next moment, a shadow moved into view.

'Lizzie, come on!'

Sorry, Mum. I'm not ready for Heaven just yet.

She kicked hard, remembering everything Hari had told her, and tore at the water with her arms. Her chest felt like it would explode, but she fought and fought, heaving herself up until with a spluttering gasp she broke the surface.

Only feet away from her, Elsie the fishergirl was holding out her hand. She was hanging over the edge of a small boat. That was what had made the shadow.

'Take my hand, Lizzie. I won't let you go.'

Lizzie clutched for Elsie's hand, held it tight and let the girl haul her on board. The fishergirl had strong brown arms, more powerful than they looked. A lifetime of hauling up fishing nets must have given her those muscles.

Lizzie spat salt water over the side of the boat, coughed and slumped in the seat. The wood below her was hot from the sun. 'Thanks,' she managed to gasp.

All around the boat, the rest of the Penny Gaff Gang

gathered. They clung onto the side and looked at her. 'Is she OK?' Dru demanded.

'I'm fine,' Lizzie said weakly. *That'll teach me*, she thought. *Try to show off in front of a boy and see where it gets you.*

'Climb aboard, you lot,' Elsie said. 'Let's get her back to the shore.'

'Yer an angel,' Lizzie groaned. 'I had a vision…'

Elsie paused, her hands on the oars. 'What's she saying?'

'Elsie, can you show us to a tea shop or something?' Malachy said, giving the others a *you-know-what-I-mean* look. 'If Lizzie's had one of her funny turns, she needs a sit down and a nice hot brew, somewhere people can't listen in.'

Elsie looked puzzled, but curious. 'Let's go and fetch your clothes off the beach. Then I'll take you back to our cottage. I knew there was more to you lot than meets the eye.'

Not long after, they were all crowded around the table in a tiny kitchen cluttered with fishing nets and lobster pots. Elsie's cottage was right beside the harbour, so close that you could look out across the sea through the diamond-leaded windows. A cat lounged there, basking in the sun, so peaceful Lizzie wondered if it had been stuffed.

Lizzie held her mug of tea in both hands as if it were the Holy Grail and breathed in the steam. She was still shaking and felt deep-down cold despite the fire Elsie had built from what little coal she had.

'You swam out too far,' Dru scolded her. 'That is how people drown, *ma cherie*. One strong cramp and – *boum!* Under the waves they go.'

'I told you, I didn't get no cramp. I had a vision!'

'I thought that's what you said!' Elsie burst out. 'You see things, don't you? Yesterday, when I was telling you about how Whitby's haunted, I thought you was laughing at me. But you're like my auntie, aren't you? She had the sight.'

'That's about the strength of it,' Lizzie said, grateful she wouldn't have to explain everything all over again. 'I tell fortunes at the circus. Only they're real fortunes, not made-up ones.'

'So what did you see?' Nora seemed keen and excited. 'Was it something about what happened at the castle?'

Oh, why did you have to say that, Lizzie thought. *I'm trying not to think of you as a suspect as it is!*

'It was a ship,' she said. 'With a green light coming off it, and all this fog rolling around it like a ruddy great cloud.'

She heard Elsie suck in a sharp breath. She wondered if she should go on. After all, she didn't want to scare the girl.

Deciding Elsie had a right to know what was going on in her town, Lizzie continued. 'There was a figure at the tiller. It was horrible – it had this long black robe, and a hood, and these two shining spots inside, like a cat's eyes.'

A frightened silence settled on the group around the table. By the window the cat stretched, yawned, got up and trotted away. The sun had gone dim, and dark clouds were rolling in from the east.

'You saw the ghost ship!' Elsie said. 'That's what I see, night after night. I never saw the *thing* at the helm, though.'

'Lucky you.'

'Do you think it were a ghost?'

'I don't know what it was.' Lizzie shuddered. She

couldn't get the memory out of her head. The way that hooded form had turned to the left and right, as if it were searching the sea … maybe Elsie's legend was true and it was hunting for a living soul to snatch away.

'Sounds like it was wearing a shroud,' Erin said. 'In County Mayo, where my gran lives, there's a man who lived by the churchyard. Every night a lady came to visit him in a long white gown. But when he finally plucked up the courage to kiss her, he saw that her gown was really a shroud! She'd been dead for over a hundred years!'

'That's nothing,' Malachy said. 'A knife-thrower who used to be with Fitzy's circus was haunted by the ghost of a man missing both his hands. It made him so scared of making a mistake he quit the circus and became a butcher!'

Soon they were all trading ghost stories around the table. It was funny, Lizzie thought, how frightening each other on purpose was better than being frightened by something from outside.

The minutes ticked by. Outside the window the sky grew steadily darker. Something covered in fur pressed up against Lizzie's ankles and she started, then realized it was only Elsie's cat. A mew came from beneath the table.

'Sorry about this,' Elsie said. 'Horatio wants feeding.'

'Horatio?' Lizzie laughed.

'Named him after Admiral Nelson, we did. I usually give him a bit of mackerel around three.'

'What? It's never three o'clock already?' Erin sprang out of her seat. 'We're going to be late for rehearsal!'

As they barged out of the little cottage and into the street, the first wet drops began to fall. The sky was completely clouded over now and the people going by hurried their steps.

Elsie stared up. 'Would you look at that sky! It's black as the Earl of Hell's waistcoat.'

'So much for our lovely day out at the beach,' said Erin.

'We're going to get soaked,' Lizzie said miserably. 'And I only just dried off properly too.'

Dru sighed. 'Well, we can't get there any faster by crying about it. Perhaps we should send for a carriage?'

Elsie laughed sharply. 'Are you made of money, Mister Frenchie?' Then, as if she regretted the jibe, she gave them a sly smile and ushered them back indoors. 'There's a way you could stay mostly dry, and it's better than any old carriage. But you'd have to promise not to tell.'

'I promise,' Lizzie said right away.

Elsie smiled to see her solemn face. 'It's not *that* grave a business. Not nowadays. But in my grandad's day, people round here would've cut your throat if you blabbed about the Rum Road.'

Now Lizzie was completely confused. 'What's a rum road?'

Nobody seemed to have any idea – except Malachy, who was suddenly grinning like a loon. 'If it's what I think it is,' he whispered to Lizzie, 'I've wanted to see one all my life.'

His excitement grew – and the others only became more confused – when Elsie fetched a candle and led them through the rainy streets to a nearby pub, the Whitby Oyster. But instead of going inside to the inviting warmth, she took them round the back to the yard.

Lizzie couldn't see any roads leading out of here. There was just a little cobbled area with some stalls for horses and a shabby wooden outhouse set against the side of the hill. To her amazement, Elsie opened the outhouse door, sparked the candle alight and beckoned them all to come and see.

Lizzie came closer and her jaw fell open. Instead of a nasty-smelling space with a plank over a hole, she saw a rough tunnel leading all the way into the hillside. The candle cast its unsteady light over the crude timbers propping the roof up and the ragged spider webs in their corners. It didn't look safe at all. In fact, it looked like something desperate men had hacked out of the earth in a hurry.

'I knew it!' Malachy crowed. 'It's a smugglers' tunnel, isn't it?'

Elsie held a finger to her lips and winked. 'Hush, lad. There's many folk gone missing and never seen again, just for blurting out our secrets.'

'Sorry.'

'Follow it all the way to the end. It comes out in a thicket not far from Dunsley Castle, within spitting distance of the road. That's where the wagons used to wait.'

'It goes *that* far?' Malachy peered into the darkness. 'That's over half a mile. Fantastic!'

Elsie passed Lizzie the candle. Lizzie cupped her hand around the fitful light, wishing they had a proper lantern to keep it safe. 'Thanks,' she said. 'You will come and see the circus, won't you?'

'Course I will!' the local girl paused. 'Did you really mean it about being a proper fortune-teller?'

Lizzie nodded.

'There's summat I need to know for sure,' Elsie said. 'I'll come and ask you. And you lot? Be careful in that tunnel.'

'It does look a bit unsteady,' Nora said. 'Should have got some honest Irish navvies on the job. It'd stand till Doomsday then.'

'I don't mean that. Whitby's a haunted place. You have to watch out if you're going into the dark. You never know what's waiting there.'

They realized she wasn't joking any more. Then, just as suddenly as the first time they'd met, she bade them goodbye and was out of sight in a second. Lizzie had the queerest feeling that Elsie might be a ghost herself.

The Penny Gaff Gang moved into the tunnel, looking around at the crumbling, cobwebbed walls and the few signs of people who'd been there before them: broken bottles, a smashed wooden cask, and a couple of old bones.

Dru poked at the bones with his foot. 'These are chewed, see?'

'Smugglers probably had dogs,' Malachy said.

'To keep watch.' He sniffed. 'That's funny. I could swear I can smell gunpowder.'

'Gunpowder?' Erin and Nora said, amazed.

'Remember that routine the clowns did last year, with the firecrackers? That's how they smelled. The smugglers must have kept a stash of powder here.'

'Last one in close the door behind you,' Lizzie murmured. She held the candle up and edged her way forward, the darkness opening up before her and returning silently in her wake. The rest of the gang followed, marvelling at the spooky atmosphere.

'We must be right under the town!' Erin said. 'Imagine if we were going under a graveyard right now. And a skeleton put its foot through the roof.'

'Oh, hush up,' Lizzie said. The air down here was musty and damp and it was all too easy to imagine ghosts up ahead, rushing towards them out of the black, their bony arms clawing. She tried to think of the living people who'd used this tunnel, not the ghosts who might be haunting it. 'Why's it called a Rum Road?'

'Because this is how they brought the rum inland,' Malachy explained. 'Tobacco too, and fancy lace. Stuff like that. But mostly rum.'

'I still don't get it.'

'Lizzie, if you bring rum into the country on a ship, you have to pay a special tax. It's called the excise. But they can't make you pay it unless they catch you with the goods. So they have special patrols looking out for anyone trying to smuggle it in.'

Suddenly it made sense. 'So this tunnel is for dodging the patrols!'

'Exactly.' Malachy ducked under an enormous spider dangling from a glistening thread. 'The smugglers could bring the rum ashore, right under the noses of the excise men.'

'What do you think, Lizzie?' asked Dru. 'Are the tunnels really haunted?'

'Elsie thinks so. I ain't about to argue with her.'

'Whoooo!' Erin hooted, wiggling her fingers in the candlelight to make long guttering shadows. 'Beware the ghost pirate of Whitby!'

'Who's walking down my old tunnel?' Nora croaked. 'Who wants their throat cut, eh?' She grabbed Malachy round the neck and he pretended she was strangling him.

Soon they were all laughing, trying to scare one another. Only Lizzie remained silent as they walked deeper and deeper into the dark. There might not be ghosts, but there was definitely *something* strange about this place.

Just as Elsie had said, the tunnel's other end was right by the road. Everybody ran the rest of the way, past the gates of the Dunsley estate and onto the lawns where the circus was pitched.

A stern-looking figure was waiting for them, looking at his watch. Fitzy. 'It's nice of you all to show up. Do you think this is a holiday?' he demanded.

'Sorry, Pop,' Malachy said. Nobody wanted to look Fitzy in the eye.

'It just won't do. Nora, Erin, Dru: you all need to be on top form for the show,' Fitzy said. 'I want you to give your very best performance for the people of Whitby. That's what the Maharaja is paying to see. So get rehearsing, or so help me I'll take my whip to you!'

As the three cast members ran off to rehearse, Fitzy turned his gaze on Malachy and Lizzie. 'Malachy, come with me. We need to work out the parade route. And you, Lizzie, can go and help Hari exercise the elephants, now he's decided to show his face again.'

Stranger and stranger, Lizzie thought as she walked over to the tents where the animal cages were kept. So it *had* been Hari she'd seen heading out to the moors, and by the sound of it, he'd been out there all day.

'Where have you been?' she demanded. 'Thought you had chores?'

'I did some exploring,' Hari said with a vague wave of his hand. 'You lead Akula if you like. I'll guide Sashi. We can take the others later. There's an ornamental lake down by the ice house where they can drink some water and cool off.'

Be like that then, Lizzie thought. *Looks like everyone's got secrets around here.* She giggled as Akula's tickly trunk nuzzled her under the arm. 'Come on then, girl. You need to stretch your legs, don't you?'

She kept a careful eye out for old Johnson as they led the two elephants down the gravel path towards the lake. If he saw that the elephants were out of their cages, he'd probably burst a blood vessel. But the gardener was nowhere to be seen.

The lake was broad and still, with a duck house on the far side and a marble statue of the Greek god Pan on a tiny island in the middle. Soon the elephants were wading gratefully into the water, splashing one another with their trunks.

'We do have permission to do this, don't we?' Lizzie asked doubtfully as they turned the huge animals loose.

'Johnson didn't say we *couldn't*,' Hari said with a grin.

'Make sure the elephants don't knock the statue over then,' she said. 'Fitzy would have to pay for a new one…' She checked over her shoulder one last time, but as there was no sign of the cantankerous groundskeeper she stretched out in the grass and closed her eyes. For the first time since this morning, when she'd nearly drowned, she felt like she could relax.

Was it only last night that she and Dru had gone dancing across these lawns? She remembered the flickering candles still burning on the banquet table, the smell of the night flowers and the gentle pressure of his arm around her waist. It was so easy to return there in her imagination. Back to the laughter and the starlight…

The sound of shouting roused her from her daydream.

The elephants were still there, sloshing around in the lake, but Hari was gone. And now she heard what the angry voice was shouting.

'Thief! Don't you try to run, you little devil. I saw what you did!'

CHAPTER 9

Only a few yards away from her, Johnson the groundskeeper held Hari firmly by the collar, lifting him up onto his tiptoes. Hari's face was flushed and Lizzie knew instantly that the man was choking him.

'I'm going to send for the police,' Johnson growled. 'No circus for you, Sonny Jim. I can spot the likes of you a mile off.'

Lizzie scrambled to her feet and ran to him. 'Let him breathe! You're strangling him!'

Johnson relaxed his grip a little but didn't let the boy go.

Hari clutched at his throat, gasping. 'Lizzie …

get Fitzy…'

'What the 'ell are you doing to him?' Lizzie yelled. 'Stop it!'

The groundskeeper blinked in surprise at Lizzie's fury. 'I'm doing my job,' he protested. 'I found this little weasel snooping around in the gardens, up to no good.'

'You're a rotten liar. You're just picking on him 'cause he's Indian!'

Johnson's mouth opened and closed but no sound came out of it. Lizzie thought he looked like an ugly fish. 'I reckon he's the thief what nicked Lady Susannah's jewels,' the groundskeeper finally managed to grunt. 'And I can prove it.'

'You're mad,' Hari gurgled. 'You've had it in for me since we came here. Admit it.'

'I saw you shovin' something black in your pocket!' Johnson shouted, shaking Hari like a terrier with a rabbit. 'It was a bit of her ladyship's jet, wasn't it? You stashed it out here, didn't you?'

'No!'

'Prove it, then,' Johnson said triumphantly. 'Turn out your pockets.'

Hari tried to wriggle free, but Johnson held his

collar tightly and grabbed his arm for good measure.

'Come on, Hari,' Lizzie said, giving Johnson a glare that could burn through steel. 'You'd better do as he says. I know you didn't steal nothing.'

'No. I won't do it,' Hari yelled. 'He can't make me.'

Lizzie stepped forward, wondering why Hari had said that. Surely he didn't have anything to hide.

'Oh, I can make you, all right!' Johnson set off towards the castle, hauling Hari with him. 'I'll drag you in front of the Maha-bloomin'-raja, and you can tell him why you've got your pockets full of his fiancée's jewels. Then we'll see what's what!'

Lizzie ran along behind the groundskeeper as he hauled Hari all the way to the front doors. He shoved them open with his shoulder, revealing a startled balding man in the hallway – the chief butler, Collins. Lizzie recognized him from the grand dinner.

'Fetch the Maharaja, Collins,' Johnson barked. 'I think he'll want to see what this little brat has been squirrelling away while his back was turned.'

'Right away,' the butler muttered through his teeth. He gave Lizzie and Hari a distasteful look. 'Perhaps the children could be taken to wait outside?'

'They won't get up to any mischief with me here to

watch 'em,' Johnson said, glowering.

'We're not thieves,' Hari snapped at him. 'You'll see.'

'Not another word out of either of you, or I'll crack your heads together!'

Collins rolled his eyes and disappeared up the great sweeping staircase. Lizzie stood quivering with anger at Johnson being so brutal and stupid. She was finally inside the magnificent castle, and she couldn't even enjoy it. The moment was ruined.

When Collins returned, he was alone. 'The Maharaja would like you to bring the young lady and gentleman up to his study, Johnson. Preferably with all their bones intact.'

Hari chose that moment to wrench himself out of Johnson's grip. He grabbed Lizzie's hand, defying the gardener to lay another finger on them. 'Lead on,' he told Collins, with a cool confidence that made Johnson even angrier.

The staircase led up past oak-panelled galleries and across a balcony. Lizzie goggled at the luxury and opulence they were walking through. Tall paintings with gilded frames loomed over her, showing serious-faced men and women in old-fashioned clothes – she couldn't guess who they were. Fresh flowers had been arranged in huge silver vases and a marble statue of a dancing Greek lady stood at the balcony's end.

What must it be like to pass by these wonderful things every single day, on your way down to breakfast? Lizzie wondered if even the knives and forks here were made from gold and silver. She supposed the Maharaja must be used to it by now. It was what he was born to, after all.

Once they seemed to have reached the very heart of the castle, Collins opened the door onto a study lined with books. Lady Susannah was sitting on the desk – Lizzie was startled at that, as it hardly seemed very ladylike – while the Maharaja paced back and forth, admiring her from different angles.

'Exquisite,' he said. 'Stupendous.'

'He's proud of her, isn't he?' Lizzie nudged Hari.

'It's not her he's talking about,' Hari said in a grim voice. 'Look at her neck.'

Lizzie looked and her eyes grew wide. Sitting on Lady Susannah's perfect white throat was a deep crimson gemstone set in a golden surround. *It has to be a paste jewel*, Lizzie thought. Because there was only one other thing it could be, and that would be impossible – surely it would be worth more than the entire castle and the grounds put together. Her mouth went dry at the thought, and a quiver went through her.

Johnson was about to speak, but the Maharaja interrupted. 'Come in, children.'

Lizzie glanced at Lady Susannah's face, hoping she was feeling well enough to have a reading from her now. She was smiling, but Lizzie could tell it was forced. *Poor thing*, she thought. *Her jet jewellery still ain't turned up, and nobody's any the wiser.*

She let her gaze drop to the gemstone. Beautiful wasn't the word for it. It turned sunlight into fire, glowing with vivid colour. This was no fake. This was a ruby, the largest one in the country. Possibly the whole world.

'You asked me, young lady, what gift I would be giving to Queen Victoria.' The Maharaja had white cotton gloves on, and he held a pointing finger up to the ruby. 'And now you can see it. The Heart of Durga. The world's largest ruby.'

Lizzie wobbled on the spot. She drank in the glorious sight with her eyes. It was so beautiful it was making her feel light-headed.

'Do you think it is beautiful?'

What a crazy question. As if anyone could think

anything different. But the Maharaja seemed totally serious, as if he genuinely cared about Lizzie's opinion. So she said, 'Oh, yes. It's the loveliest thing I've ever clapped eyes on.'

'It is a priceless treasure of India,' Hari said.

Lizzie caught her breath. She could hear cold anger in Hari's voice. The Maharaja beamed, thinking he was being polite, completely missing his rage.

'Priceless? You should lock it up, then!' exploded Johnson. 'Especially with this little thief about.'

Lady Susannah's smile vanished. 'I beg your pardon?'

'I caught 'im snooping around in the gardens by himself. Looking for a place to hide the jewels he stole, no doubt, so he wouldn't get caught with them on his person.'

'You think this boy stole her ladyship's jet?' frowned the Maharaja. 'But where is your proof? Small boys love to explore gardens. When I was a boy I was always climbing up trees and digging in the dirt.'

'I saw him putting summat in his pocket,' the groundskeeper insisted. 'Summat black and shiny! You tell me that ain't Whitby jet he was squirrelling away.'

'I dunno what you think you saw, but Hari's no thief,' Lizzie yelled angrily. 'He's my friend, and he's kind and gentle, and he's nicer than you could ever be!'

The Maharaja clapped his hands briskly. 'I will have silence.' It was the voice of a man who was used to being obeyed. Everyone did as he commanded, even Johnson. 'Young man,' the Maharaja told Hari, 'please forgive the imposition, but I must ask you to turn out your pockets.'

Hari shrugged. 'All you had to do was ask politely.' He emptied his pockets onto the Maharaja's desk, producing a fistful of peanuts, some string, a large tooth from who knew what animal, and finally a shiny black stone.

The Maharaja picked it up and turned it around with interest. His eyebrows rose as he saw the form of a snail-like creature embedded in the rock. 'What a magnificent specimen. Can you tell me what it is?'

'It's an ammonite,' Hari said.

The Maharaja laughed. '"Fossil" would have done perfectly well.' His body shook. He was bubbling over with laughter now. 'Oh dear, Mister Johnson. Oh dear me. I am afraid your sleuthing skills fall rather short of the mark.' Hands on hips, he roared with laughter until he had to stop, lean against the desk and wipe his eyes. 'Whitby jet, indeed.'

'May I have my fossil back now, please?' Hari asked.

'Ah. Since you found it on the castle grounds, it is technically *my* fossil, but let's not quibble over it, eh? Johnson, give the young lad his treasure back. And I think you owe him an apology too.'

'Sorry,' grumbled Johnson, not even looking at Hari. He quickly added, 'But I had your best interests at heart, Your Excellency. And I've looked after these gardens for years. You can't expect me to let young hooligans go tearin' through them any which way they please.'

The Maharaja crossed the room to the window and put his hands behind his back. 'You do a splendid job, Johnson. The gardens are quite magnificent...' His voice trailed off.

'Is something wrong?' Lady Susannah asked.

'Ahem. Johnson, you might want to get back to the gardens. There appear to be a pair of elephants trampling through your geraniums.'

'*Elephants!?*' Johnson jumped in the air as if he'd been jabbed in the backside. He pushed past Hari and Lizzie and ran down the corridor, nearly knocking Collins the butler off the balcony on his way.

Lizzie ran to the window to see. It was no joke.

Without Hari there to watch them, the elephants had clambered out of the ornamental pond and were lumbering in a straight line towards their enclosure, ploughing through everything in their path.

Johnson's despairing cry drifted up the stairs. Moments later, they saw him running out across the lawn, flailing his arms wildly.

'Hmm,' said the Maharaja. 'Elephants don't appreciate being shouted at. Despite his temper, Johnson is a good gardener. I would hate for him to be trampled flat on his own lawn. You two had better go and round them up.'

'Right you are, Your Excellency,' Lizzie said, dropping into a curtsey.

'I can't wait for the parade this evening,' the Maharaja said with a giggle. He was still as full of joy as any child would be. 'In fact, watching those elephants roaming about has given me a capital idea…'

'Dare I ask?' said Lady Susannah, raising an eyebrow. He leaned close and whispered something in her ear. Lady Susannah's eyes widened in surprise and she giggled.

Lizzie took that as her cue to leave.

Soon after, she and Hari were leading two happy

elephants back to their pens. Fitzy, to Lizzie's relief, took their side. If Johnson was daft enough to drag the animal handler off and leave the elephants unsupervised, what did he expect to happen? Besides, the Maharaja had been very understanding, so no more need be said about it.

'He's such a nice man,' Lizzie said to Hari.

'Who? Fitzy?'

'No, the Maharaja. He's the sweetest toff I ever met.'

'Sweet?' Hari scowled. 'He's no better than a thief. How dare he steal that ruby from India and give it to Queen Victoria, as if it was his to give away? And he has the gall to fret when someone steals from him!'

Suddenly, Lizzie wondered if it *was* Hari who had stolen the jet jewellery. To her the jet had seemed like it was worth a fortune, but that was before she'd seen the Heart of Durga. To someone whose country had lost such a treasure, surely stealing one necklace in revenge was a mere drop in the ocean…

CHAPTER 10

Making things with her hands always made Lizzie feel better. Back in the days when she lived in Rat's Castle, she'd made paper flowers from coloured streamers to sell from a tray on the street. She was as quick and neat as any seamstress, with nimble fingers that would have made her an excellent pickpocket if her life had taken a different direction.

Now she sat in her caravan and threaded the shells she'd collected onto black cord. With a gimlet she'd borrowed from one of the handymen, she'd made holes in them so the cockleshells would lie flat. Two identical necklaces steadily took shape.

'My bonnie lies over the ocean,' she sang as she worked. 'My bonnie lies over the sea…' Erin and Nora would love their bracelets, she knew. Maybe, if she had a few rich clients come for readings, she'd be able to buy a couple of beads of real Whitby jet and add them as spacers between the bigger shells. It might not be a whole jet necklace, but it ought to make Nora happy.

For all you know, Nora's got Lady Susannah's necklace stashed somewhere, whispered a nasty voice at the back of her mind. *Maybe Nora and Hari stole it together…*

Lizzie chatted nonsense to herself to keep the suspicious thoughts away. '"She sells seashells on the sea shore." Well, that's daft, innit? Who's going to buy seashells on the sea shore? There's loads of 'em lying about. Silly moo.'

She was proudly laying out the finished bracelets on her dressing table when the distant boom of a gong rang out from the show tent.

'That's the parade getting ready to start!' she said in a panic. 'Blimey, where'd the time go?' She set off at a run towards the show tent, where lines of circus folk were already forming. Then, thinking again, she changed direction and ran to the tea tent. The parade would take hours, and she hadn't eaten all day.

The tea-tent door flaps were usually pegged open, but now they were hanging down, blocking her path. Surely Ma Sullivan hadn't closed up shop already? Lizzie wrestled her way through.

Ma Sullivan was there, and so were Nora and Erin, all bending over something. The twins bounced up like jackrabbits, grinning all over their faces, while Ma Sullivan rummaged around behind the counter. Lizzie saw she was shoving something out of sight.

'Hello, Lizzie me love,' Ma Sullivan said, standing up and wiping her brow. All three of them were grinning like toy monkeys. 'Here for a quick bowl of stew before we leave?'

'Please,' Lizzie said, eyeing them suspiciously.

Nora and Erin watched her take her seat. Neither spoke. Lizzie's thoughts were racing now. What could possibly be going on? All the Sullivans seemed to be acting shifty. There was one explanation, and she didn't want to dwell on it, but she couldn't help it. It came back to her, just like it had in her caravan.

She'd seen Nora fastening a jet necklace around her neck. Her visions were *never* wrong. Whether she'd stolen the necklace herself or not, it seemed she must have it now. And who could Nora trust not to betray her, out of the whole circus? Her mother and sister, of course.

Were Ma Sullivan and Erin in on it too?

She banished the thought as a smiling Ma Sullivan served her up a brimming bowl of stew and a big hunk of bread to sop it up with. 'Get that down you, dear. But don't bolt it now. You've a good quarter hour before the parade sets off and I don't want you getting indigestion.'

Lizzie tucked in, though she wasn't feeling very hungry now. Her stomach squirmed like a live oyster being doused in lemon juice. Lately it seemed her visions were bringing her more pain than joy. If she hadn't seen Nora putting that necklace on, she'd still be happy and trusting, with no idea anything might be wrong. Now she had no choice but to be suspicious of her friends who had become like sisters to her.

And she hated it.

The parade was nearly ready to set off for town. Fitzy, in a red spangled jacket and brandishing a golden baton, strode up and down inspecting the circus performers who were lined up on the castle courtyard. From the silk-draped elephants in front to the trapeze artists in spangles at the back, everyone was wearing their very best costumes. They all held handfuls of flyers, ready to throw out to the public.

Lizzie grinned to see all her friends in the procession. There was the band in the middle, ready to march. The clowns were going through warm-up exercises, doing star jumps and press-ups in full make-up. Leo, the circus lion, paced back and forth in his cage. All the Sullivan boys were astride their ponies, handsome in their Wild West gear, while Erin and Nora had quickly changed into their Bareback Balleta dresses. Everywhere, colours shone out more brightly than Johnson's flowers – scarlet and gold, silver-blue and rich green.

Then, without warning, the castle doors boomed open and a figure came striding out, every bit as colourful as the parade. It was Gurinder Bhatti, wearing a traditional silk outfit and a splendid turban. Lizzie felt a jolt of excitement as she saw the Heart of Durga gleaming from the turban's front.

'Look at you all!' cried the Maharaja. 'You are magnificent. Oh, happy day when I invited you to visit us in Whitby.'

'The honour is all ours,' Fitzy said with a polite bow. 'I take it you'll be watching the parade with the Lord Mayor and his wife?'

'Watch it?' the Maharaja said in horror. 'My dear man, I wish to be *in* the parade!'

Fitzy coughed into his fist. 'Naturally. Perhaps you would like to lead it alongside me?'

'I shall ride on one of the elephants,' Gurinder Bhatti announced. 'That one.' He was pointing at Akula.

Hari held her guiding rope and glanced up at his uncle. 'I'm afraid that would not be a good idea,' Zezete said smoothly. 'The elephants do not know you, sir. A parade can be a noisy business and they need to know their rider for such an occasion. Their trust has to be earned.'

'Pah,' the Maharaja snorted. 'I have ridden elephants countless times. Probably more than you, in fact. There's nothing to it.' He walked to Akula's side and tugged on the ropes holding her howdah secure. Lizzie remembered that word from when Hari had first helped her climb aboard Akula – a howdah was a sort of padded seat that perched on an elephant's back.

Fitzy tried to protest, but the Maharaja waved

him away. 'I insist. Please don't fuss. I do know what I'm doing.'

He was going to get his own way, Lizzie knew. For some reason, that made her feel nervous. She didn't like the way Zezete and Hari were glaring at him, and she knew that the elephants got upset when people argued and shouted. Like many animals, they could pick up on a mood, and it could make them touchy.

Then, sudden as a bullet through her head, it came: a vision. She clenched her eyes shut and stood with her fists balled, shaking as if she were having a fit.

She saw the Maharaja on top of an elephant, smiling and waving. The girl leading the elephant through the crowded Whitby streets was Lizzie herself! The next moment, the elephant trumpeted and reared up. Screams rang out and people began to panic.

'Don't!' she cried out at the top of her voice.

The Maharaja was already perched on Akula's back. Silence fell. Everyone stared at Lizzie. She stood, shaking and breathless, the centre of attention.

'I beg your pardon?' the Maharaja said.

'Don't ride on Akula,' Lizzie begged. But even as she spoke, she struggled to find the right words. How could she possibly convince him? If she said she'd had a vision, he'd probably laugh in her face. A superstitious local girl like Elsie might take her visions seriously, but surely not someone as rich and powerful as Gurinder Bhatti.

'It's ... such a long way down,' she stammered. 'What if you fell off? What if Akula threw you? You could be hurt – hurt terrible.'

The Maharaja wasn't angry. 'Dear girl, you do not know elephants as I do. This elephant is as gentle as any lamb.'

Hari shrugged and offered Lizzie Akula's guiding rope. 'Want to lead her?' he said quietly, so nobody else could hear. 'She trusts you.'

Lizzie thought quickly. *If I'm not leading her, then the vision can't come true! All I have to do is lead a different elephant and the Maharaja will be safe!*

'No, you take Akula,' she said. 'She loves you more than any of us. I'll lead Sashi.'

'Suit yourself,' Hari said, looking at her oddly.

Lizzie felt clever that she'd thought of a way to avert disaster as the procession began to move off.

* * *

The plan was for the parade to head along the coast road, down the zigzag pathways into town and across the swing bridge over the River Esk. The acrobats and jugglers would put on a little show, then everyone would troop back across the bridge and up the coast towards Dunsley Castle again.

Lizzie led Sashi the elephant towards the end of the bridge, where a huge crowd had gathered. 'Brilliant idea to cross the river,' Malachy said, keeping pace with her. 'Nice and high up, no buildings in the way to block the view. They'll be able to see us for miles around.'

'This bridge will take an elephant's weight, won't it?' Lizzie wondered.

'We'll soon find out,' Malachy said, grinning. He jumped up and down on the spot. 'Seems sturdy enough to me.'

'Here they come!' Lizzie heard a child shout.

The crowds chatted excitedly and pointed as they heard the blast of trumpets and the booming of a big bass drum. The parade rounded the curve of the street, with the Maharaja in the front, riding on Akula and waving. By the look of it, the whole town had turned out to see them. Children rode on shoulders and fishermen stood on the decks of their boats.

'There's Elsie!' Lizzie waved frantically. The fishergirl was watching with her entire family from their little boat. She caught Lizzie's eye and waved back.

'And there's Lady Susannah,' Malachy said. Fan in hand, the lady was watching the parade approach from the near end of the bridge, where some other posh-looking people were standing. 'Shame there's no royal box, eh?'

'There's the Mayor and Mayoress too. Look at his big gold chain. It don't look like much next to the Maharaja's ruby, though, does it? And there's … *Billy?*'

Lizzie stared as the seaside con man came sidling up to the group of toffs. *He must be getting ready to pick a pocket*, she thought. And he'd probably be successful too, as they were all watching the circus parade and acting as if he wasn't there. Posh people always did that, Lizzie knew – anything common or vulgar, they just pretended they couldn't see it.

Now Billy was moving in on Lady Susannah. Lizzie stiffened to see him strut up to her like that, his hands in his pockets, as if he were the king of the whole town.

Her ladyship produced her big black feathery fan and held it in front of her face, like a barrier. It didn't stop Billy. He leaned in and began to whisper in her ear. There was something sickening about his oily grin. Lady Susannah looked trapped, fluttering her fan nervously.

'Malachy, look!'

'I see him. What a bloomin' liberty. We can't let that weasel mess about with the Maharaja's lady friend!'

As they approached the group of dignitaries, Lizzie bellowed, 'Oi! Leave the lady alone!'

Billy jumped, as if he'd been caught robbing a safe. Lady Susannah was startled, but looked grateful to see them, and gave the children a smile and a little wave.

'I don't think the lady appreciates your attention,' Malachy yelled to Billy.

'Sling yer hook!' Lizzie snapped, jerking her thumb.

Billy shrugged. 'Can't blame me for trying,' he called, giving them a wink. Whistling a jaunty tune, he slipped off into the crowd without a backward glance.

Lady Susannah's cheeks were flushed as she fanned herself. 'You are heroes, the pair of you,' she called. 'Thank you for rescuing me from that dreadful man.'

By now, the front of the parade was moving out over the bridge. Lizzie watched nervously as the two elephants lumbered through the crowd, with the Maharaja flinging pamphlets like confetti to the left and right. 'Roll up, roll up,' he shouted. 'Spectacular circus tomorrow night! Bring the family!'

'He looks like he's wanted to do this all his life,' Lizzie said to Malachy.

In the midst of the noise and chaos, Hari beckoned Lizzie over. She gave Malachy Sashi's lead to hold and walked to the head of the procession.

'I need a favour,' he muttered. 'Take Akula's rope and lead her for a moment, would you? I'll be right back.'

'What?' Cold panic took hold of her. If she was leading Akula, then the vision could come true after all. 'I can't!'

'It's only for a moment,' Hari insisted. 'I have a quick errand I need to do in town. Please, Lizzie? It's really important and I might not get another chance.'

Lizzie reluctantly took Akula's rope. 'You'd better come straight back,' she warned.

Hari ran off immediately. He weaved in and out of the bystanders, making for the rows of shops beyond the harbour. 'Some bloomin' errand,' Lizzie muttered to herself. 'Looks more like a shopping trip to me.'

Lizzie walked at the very front of the procession, leading Akula and feeling more and more nervous.

At least the elephant was peaceful and content. Lizzie stroked her cheek as they walked. 'Good girl,' she whispered.

The Maharaja, high above, waved wildly to the crowd. 'Ladies and gentlemen! Come one, come all, to Fitzy's Circus of Wonders and Marvels!'

Just then, a harsh voice from the crowd yelled out, 'Go home! You don't belong here!'

Lizzie glanced around to see who had spoken. Then from out of the crowd a rock came hurtling through the air, arching over the tops of people's heads. It struck Akula's side with a thud. Lizzie screamed and Akula trumpeted in pain. The elephant flung her head to the left and right and Lizzie fought to hold onto her rope, but it was no use. Her vision was coming true and there was nothing she could do to stop it.

More screams rang out from the crowd and people ran for cover as the maddened elephant reared up...

CHAPTER 11

The elephant trumpeted and raged like something from an ancient battle. One man dived over the side of the bridge and fell into the river as Akula's head swung towards him. The crowd up ahead screamed and ran, cramming against one another in their haste to get out of the way.

'It's going to charge!' someone screamed. 'We'll all be killed!'

Akula's front legs came down on the bridge. Lizzie felt the whole thing shiver under her feet and that sent a fresh wave of panic through the crowd – Malachy had been sure the bridge would take an elephant's weight, but a panicked elephant?

Sashi stood, twitching his trunk nervously as Akula reared up again, her legs waving. The Maharaja clung on, one hand clutching the howdah straps and the other pressed to his head. Of course, Lizzie thought – he's scared the turban with the ruby in it will fall off.

'She ain't going to charge,' Lizzie yelled. She still had hold of the rope, which tugged and strained in her grip as Akula thrashed about. 'She's gentle, she just had a fright.'

Nobody listened. Lizzie stood her ground as screaming people ran past her. The end of the bridge was bottlenecked with the escaping crowd now, pressed so tight they were crushing one another. People were running up to see what was happening and getting in the way of the ones who were trying to leave. It was total chaos.

There was a bloody mark on Akula's side where the rock had hit her. The crowd was making it worse, Lizzie knew. The poor elephant was panicking, feeling trapped and threatened.

In that moment, Lizzie knew Akula *would* charge if she had to. She didn't know any better. She needed to feel safe, and would plough through a crowd to get away if that was what it took.

'I've got to do something,' she gasped. Zezete was further down at the other end of the bridge with the lion. He was running up to help, pushing his way through the crowd, but couldn't possibly reach her in time. Hari had run off heaven only knew where. She had to try.

She reached for Akula's trunk. The elephant's massive feet came down almost on top of her, but she forced herself to stand still and to sing. She tried to sound like Hari, with lots of up-and-down notes. She didn't know the words to his Indian songs, so she just threw in words she did know instead. '*My bonnie lies over the oo-ooo-oocean, my bonnie lies over the see-eee-ea...*'

Akula hesitated and swung her great barrel-like head down.

Very gently, Lizzie reached up and stroked her trunk, and when the elephant didn't flinch away, she stroked it again. '*Oh bring back my bonnie to meeee,*' she sang softly. 'And bring a great big bag of peanuts for the best elephant in the world.'

Without being asked, Akula knelt down. The look in her eye seemed to say sorry. The crowds began to settle down, murmuring, as they saw what was going on. 'Why, it's all a trick!' one man yelled angrily. 'Part of the show. That girl was in control of the beast all the time.'

'Nothing but a cheap stunt,' someone else sneered.

Down below, in the river, the man who had dived in was hauling himself onto the shore. He wrung out his cloth cap, shrugged and put it back on his head.

'Lizzie, what's going on?' Hari came running back, dodging in and out of the people milling aimlessly on the bridge. He was shoving a parcel into his pocket, wrapped in brown paper. 'I heard Akula trumpeting. Is she all right?'

'She's fine *now*, no ruddy thanks to you!' Lizzie angrily handed him the guiding rope. 'I hope your "errand" was important. Someone could have been killed!'

'Akula would never hurt anyone.'

'Not on purpose. But someone chucked a rock at her, didn't they? She nearly threw the Maharaja off her back.' She turned to him. 'Are you all right up there, sir?'

The Maharaja waved away her concerns. 'I am quite well,' he said, though his hands were shaking and his turban was crooked.

'You'd better get down and walk the rest of the way,' Hari suggested.

'Out of the question. I began this parade on an elephant, and I shall finish it on an elephant. If anyone has anything to say to me, they can say it to my face!'

As the parade began to move off again, through a muttering and agitated crowd, Lizzie found she rather admired the man's pride. He might be silly in some ways, but he was brave with it. For all he knew, someone was still out there getting ready to throw another rock.

Lizzie wondered who had thrown the first one. She looked over the faces of the crowd, trying to spot anyone who looked angry or hateful. Then she glanced at Hari walking by her side, and another possibility came to mind.

It could have been Hari. He's no friend of the Maharaja's, is he? Hasn't he said, again and again, what a thief and a traitor he thinks he is? And wasn't it ever so convenient that Hari had to rush off on an 'errand', just before the rock was thrown?

'Shut up,' she whispered to her own suspicious thoughts.

It could have been him. You can't prove it wasn't.

'Yes I can,' Lizzie told herself triumphantly. 'It don't

matter how much Hari hates the Maharaja. He'd never, ever hurt Akula just to put him in danger. He loves that elephant.'

Malachy frowned and glanced her way. 'Who are you muttering to over there?'

'Just talking to myself,' Lizzie said with a sigh. 'First sign of madness. Ain't that what they say?'

The setting sun was turning the waves red by the time Lizzie, Erin and Nora finally returned to the castle grounds.

'That could have gone a lot worse,' Lizzie said. 'Akula calmed down pretty quick, and the crowd liked the jugglers. And when Sardini did his fire-eating they thought it were the Devil himself!'

'Do you reckon we'll get a big turnout tomorrow?' Erin yawned.

'If we don't, it's their loss,' said Nora. 'The show's free, so people have nothing to lose by coming along.'

'We'll give 'em the best show we can, and if they don't like it, they can go jump off a cliff,' Erin said.

'Hear hear,' Lizzie said with a grin.

'So the sideshows and penny gaffs had better get them properly warmed up!' Nora said, stretching. 'That means you, Lizzie. Send them into the show tent with their eyes good and wide.'

Lizzie reached her caravan and held the door open. 'Right. Cocoa and gossip time, girls. You two fetch the drinks, and I'll get the candles lit and fluff the cushions up.'

'Ah, not tonight, eh?' Erin yawned. 'Me arms and legs are dropping off, I'm that tired.'

Lizzie couldn't believe what she was hearing. Cocoa and gossip was a nightly ritual. They *always* got together in Old Jemima for a before-bedtime chat, about boys and future plans and the dreams they all had.

'Me too,' said Nora. 'Big day tomorrow. We should get an early night. Lots of rest. Sleep well, Lizzie, see ya in the morning.'

Lizzie felt like her world had been shaken to the foundations. One twin snubbing their get-together was bad enough, but *both*?

'Oh well, don't let me keep you up or nothing,' she said, turning her back on them.

She shut the caravan door with a bang. Then she sat on the bed, her head in her hands, and tried not to cry. Lizzie felt something lumpy underneath her. She pulled out the shell bracelets she'd made, hidden under the quilt so Erin and Nora wouldn't see them when they came over.

'Needn't have bothered,' she sniffed. She flung them under the bed, threw herself onto the pillow and shut her eyes to the world. If everyone else was having an early night, she'd have one too.

The day of the gala performance dawned, and Lizzie woke from blessedly dreamless sleep.

Preparations were already in full swing. Like a great clockwork machine with all its parts in good order, the circus went to work. Everyone had to keep up the pace; there was no time for any one member to fret or lag behind. Rehearsals that had filled the days before were given a final polish. Costumes were checked for any stray threads or last-minute darning. Lions, elephants and camels were groomed until they seemed bright and new as the figures on a Noah's Ark toy.

Finally, with an hour left to go, Fitzy gathered everyone on the castle lawn. Excitement seethed in the crowd. The circus folk couldn't wait to get cracking, and Fitzy knew it. Lizzie grinned at him as he made his way up to his soapbox.

'Look at you all, fizzing like the bubbles in a bottle of champagne,' he laughed. 'Let's give the bottle an extra shake or two before we pop the cork, shall we?'

The circus folk laughed and cheered. Fitzy lifted his hat to them.

'When I was just a little boy, playing at circuses under the table, I promised myself one day I'd put on a show for the King himself. Well, this is the next best thing, folks. The Maharaja Gurinder Bhatti – Queen Victoria's chum! Maybe this time next year we'll be at Buckingham Palace!'

In that moment, Lizzie could believe it. She wondered if she'd get to do a reading for the Queen. Maybe she could speak to her dead husband, Albert, and comfort her in her hour of grief…

'But among all these la-di-dah high society types, my dears,' Fitzy went on, 'I want you to remember why we're in this business in the first place. It doesn't matter how many kings and queens you have in your audience. What matters is this: you have the power to make every single person watching *feel* like a king or queen. That's a rare and precious thing. I want to see royal smiles everywhere I look, is that understood? Work your magic today, ladies and gents. Make me proud.'

The crowd cheered, then broke up, boiling over with excitement. Lizzie ran across the lawn to her caravan as if she was running across the clouds in the sky.

It was circus custom to open the sideshows and 'penny gaffs' some hours before the main performance, to warm the crowd up and bring in some extra money on top of ticket sales. That was where Lizzie's job came in. Of course, they wouldn't be paying her today, as the Maharaja had already agreed a handsome fee with Fitzy for the whole setup – for the people of Whitby the whole show was free, sideshows and all.

She changed into her scarlet and gold clairvoyant's robes, which were long and rather baggy so she could pull them on top of her regular clothes if she had to. Ma Sullivan had sewn them for her after the old ones her predecessor Madame Aurora had worn had finally become too threadbare for use. A gauzy veil over her face completed the ensemble.

Her fortune-telling tent stood by the main entrance to the castle grounds, with her hand-painted wooden sign propped outside. *The Magnificent Lizzie Brown,* it declared. *Genuine Clairvoyant – Thousands of Testimonials – Eighth Wonder of the World.* Lizzie wasn't quite sure what the other seven wonders of the world were supposed to be, but thought Akula was probably one of them.

Inside, the tent was cosy and a bit stuffy. All her props were in a wicker case where the circus porters had left them for her. One by one, she took them out and put them in place: velvet cloth on the round table, crystal ball and incense burner on the side table, Tarot cards spread out in a fan shape, a little ivory statue of a fat Chinese bloke next to them.

Lizzie loved setting up her tent. It had become a little ritual to her, her way of feeling at home in a new city or campsite. The last thing to do was light the incense. Curling grey tongues of sandalwood smoke wafted into the darkened air. It wasn't that these props heightened her psychic abilities, but her customers expected a mystical atmosphere – so she gave it to them. She sat back, smiling behind her veil, and waited for the first customer to appear.

Sure enough, one did. A curly head popped around the tent door. 'Y'all right, Liz? It's me, Elsie. Is it you under all that get-up?'

'Come in,' Lizzie said, 'and let the tent flap down behind you. You said you wanted to know something for sure?'

Elsie shivered as she sat down. 'It's the ghost ship,' she whispered. 'I couldn't say before, because I didn't know if I could trust you. But ... I think I know who it is.'

Lizzie's mind flashed back to the hooded figure looming over the bright green light, with fog billowing all around it.

'I think it's my brother,' Elsie said.

Lizzie frowned. 'What, playing tricks or something?'

'My *dead* brother.'

Suddenly Lizzie understood what she meant. Of course – this was a fishing town, and tragedies at sea surely happened all the time. 'When did he ... pass away?'

'Three years ago. He was lost at sea. They never found a trace of him, nor of his ship, the *Green Linnet*. Jack Hodgkins and Selwyn Booth, his mates, they was lost too.'

'I'm sorry,' Lizzie said. But Elsie's eyes were dry. Lizzie got the feeling Elsie had already shed all the tears she would cry for her brother, long ago. The people up here weren't soft.

'Can you talk to him? If he's not at rest – if it's *him* haunting Whitby harbour and keeping me awake at night – then I want to know why.'

Unfinished business, Lizzie thought to herself. Ghosts who still had something left to do on earth couldn't cross over to the afterlife. Like Jacob Hayward back in Kensal Green, whose corpse had been dug up by body-snatchers.

'I can talk to the dead, if they're willing,' Lizzie said. 'But I need something to make a connection. Have you got anything that belonged to him?'

Elsie silently put a clay pipe on the table between them. Lizzie saw it was still stuffed with old, unsmoked tobacco. 'I used to fill it for him every night, so he could have his smoke when he came in from sea,' Elsie said, her voice catching a little. 'Didn't have the heart to throw it away, did I?'

'Just as well you didn't,' Lizzie said. She held the pipe in her cupped hands – it was still warm from Elsie's body – and closed her eyes.

Instantly she was somewhere else. Bright sunshine in a clear blue sky, and waves dancing below her feet – she was hovering, weightless, out on the open sea.

A woman, wearing a dress made from shiny scales and with seaweed twisted through her long, greenish hair, rose up from the sea.

'Why are you here?' she said. 'Who do you seek, child who walks between the worlds?'

'I'm looking for Elsie's brother,' Lizzie told it.

The figure shook her head. 'Matt Towersey is not here, child. Nor is Jack Hodgkins, nor Selwyn Booth. Gone from the world of men are they. They sing and laugh together in Fiddler's Green.'

With a gasp, Lizzie was suddenly back in her tent. She could still see the after-image of the ethereal figure behind her eyes.

'What did you see?' Elsie demanded, her voice rising. 'The ghost – is it him?'

'I … I spoke to someone,' Lizzie said, feeling shaken. 'It was some sort of an ocean spirit, I think. A kindly one. It said Matt Towersey was in Fiddler's Green.'

When she heard those words, Elsie clapped her hands to her cheeks and the tears began to flow. 'I never told you his name!'

'I don't think your brother's the ghost on the ship,' Lizzie said carefully.

'He's not.' Elsie was certain now. 'Not if he's in Fiddler's Green. He always used to joke about that lovely place... You've never heard of it, have you?'

'No. Sorry.'

Elsie wiped her eyes. 'It's the sailors' paradise. Bad sailors go down to Davy Jones's Locker, but the good ones go to Fiddler's Green, until they're ready to go to Heaven. The stories say you see your old friends there, and the ale never runs dry.'

'So his soul's at peace.'

'Aye, and thank God for that.' Elsie stood up, looking worried. 'It's my own soul I've got to worry about now.'

'What do you mean?' Lizzie couldn't understand why the girl wasn't more cheerful. She thought she'd given her *good* news.

'That ghost ship's still out there, in't it? If it's not my brother's ghost, then whose is it?'

For the next two hours, Lizzie read palms and answered questions. All the girls wanted to know if their sweethearts would come back to them, all the boys wanted to know if they would be rich … it was the same old story, just with different names and faces.

She was getting better at telling people the truth without upsetting them, though. All you had to do was focus on the good things you saw. There was always something, if you looked hard enough – even if it was just the chance to turn aside bad luck before it happened.

Lizzie sat up, startled, as Lady Susannah entered her tent. The lady sat down opposite her and gave a tight smile. Out came the fan, wafting away the incense smoke.

'Sorry,' Lizzie said. 'It's a bit thick, I know.'

'I don't usually believe in this sort of thing,' the lady said, her voice a low murmur. 'But I have watched person after person come out of this tent, singing your praises. So I am willing to try.'

'You want to know about your jewellery?' Excitement seized Lizzie. Finally, a chance to find out the truth and put suspicion to rest!

'Ha! Oh, no. This is something far more important.'

Lizzie opened her mouth and shut it again. 'You'd better give me your hand, then. The left one.'

'Wait. I want you to swear, on your mother's grave,

that you'll never tell anyone what you see. Not a soul, you understand?'

'I promise,' Lizzie whispered. She had the feeling of being on the edge of a cliff again. Only the slightest push, and she would go over...

Lady Susannah licked her lips and took Lizzie's hands in a tight grip. Her fingers were cold and smooth. 'Tell me whether my Maharaja will marry me.'

'Ohhh,' Lizzie said. 'Now I understand.' Lady Susannah, for all her finery and posh manners, was no different from the fishing girls from the village.

The lady frowned, then broke into a wide smile. 'Yes. Clever girl. I am quite head over heels in love, and I am *desperate* to marry him. But he's not asked me yet, and I fear he never will. Is that silly of me?'

'Course it's not!' *Just another girl with a sweetheart problem*, Lizzie thought. 'Let's be having you, then. Er ... my lady.'

She stroked her finger down Lady Susannah's line of life. Images began to appear, as they always did. She saw a happy little blonde girl riding on a pony while a second sour-faced girl, blonde like the first, jealously watched.

When Lizzie described the image, Lady Susannah

nodded eagerly. 'Jennifer Meadows always hated me,' she smirked. 'I showed her, though. Now hurry up and show me the future.'

More childhood scenes followed: a party, a girl running in tears from a clown, a kitten with a ribbon around its neck. As she saw the scenes, Lizzie described to Lady Susannah what she was seeing.

Then, without warning, a horrible scene appeared.

Lady Susannah was a young woman now, staring up in terror as above her loomed a swarthy man in a long robe, holding a huge curved sword.

He laughed, as if he relished her fear. 'Time to die, my pretty!'

Then there was a bright flash, Lady Susannah screamed, and the sword came plunging down…

CHAPTER 12

'What?' Lady Susannah demanded.

'Someone tried to kill you!' Lizzie said, horrified. 'A man with a big sharp sword. He was standing over you and laughing. How did you escape? Did the police catch him?'

This wasn't filling in missing pieces of the puzzle. This was just making the puzzle even more baffling. Who would want to kill Lady Susannah? Lizzie could understand stealing from her – the jet was worth a fortune – but murder? Possibilities raced through her mind. Maybe the Maharaja had enemies who would never let him marry an English woman. Or maybe a group of assassins had come over from India, wanting revenge on him and his family?

Lady Susannah snatched her hand away. 'Those unpleasant incidents are in the *past*,' she said, as if Lizzie had done something stupid. 'I believe I asked you to tell me about my future?'

'Sorry,' Lizzie mumbled. 'I'll do me best.'

She took Lady Susannah's hand again. Straightaway, a vision stood out in her mind. It was bright and perfectly clear, which told Lizzie it was the future she was seeing. But the vision was even worse than the last.

'Do you see my wedding day?' Lady Susannah asked eagerly. 'What time of year is it? Are there leaves on the trees? Hurry up, I want to know.'

But what Lizzie saw was no wedding. Lady Susannah, her hair in disarray, was wearing a dirty, ripped grey dress and her hands were bound behind her back. She was weeping and struggling to escape from her bonds. 'Please don't kill me,' she pleaded to her unseen captor.

'Someone's going to try to murder you,' Lizzie gasped.

'Didn't I tell you not to look at the past?'

'It's not the past! You were all dirty and ragged. I saw your hands – there wasn't a wedding ring on your finger. You're not going to get married, you're going to get killed!'

'Oh, for heaven's sake.' Lady Susannah slammed her hand down on the table, rattling the crystal balls. 'Do I look like a schoolgirl? You and your little friends may enjoy titillating one another with penny-dreadful tales of blood and gore, but the rest of us have outgrown such stuff. What a cruel, juvenile prank!'

'But that's what I saw! I'm sorry, but he ain't never going to marry you, and—'

'Adamant, are we? Very well. I see I shall have to have words with your employer about this.' She stormed out of the tent, leaving Lizzie with the mental image of her weeping and struggling.

'But your life's in danger, yer ladyship!' Lizzie protested. It was no good. She was already gone – and by the look of it, any customers who were still waiting had taken off too. Of course; they wouldn't want to risk having a reading with the Magnificent Lizzie Brown if Lady Susannah didn't approve.

Lizzie sat, her stomach churning with nerves, and wondered what she should do. Clearly, some danger from her past had returned to stalk Lady Susannah in the present. Someone, possibly the same person who wanted to hurt the Maharaja, meant to kill her. And they would strike soon.

The more she thought about it, the more Lizzie realized she hadn't broken the news to Lady Susannah very politely. '"You were all dirty and ragged,"' she muttered to herself. 'Just the sort of thing a lady wants to hear. Flippin' heck.' Perhaps she should have just said her life was in danger, and then added the details if she'd been pressed for them.

She should apologize. Lizzie rushed out into the crowd, trying to see where Lady Susannah had gone. There was no sign of her.

She knocked on the Sullivans' caravan door. It was a little ajar, so she opened it the rest of the way and popped her head round. 'Almost show time!'

The girls were sprawled on the floor. Lizzie saw the caravan's bellybox was open and the sewing kit was out. Before she could see what they'd been working on, Erin slammed the bellybox lid down. 'Have you not got customers waiting?' she said in surprise.

'All done. I'm free as a bird.'

Lizzie looked at the twins, and the twins looked at Lizzie. 'All right, then,' she said at length. 'Own up. What are you making in here? And don't say "nothing", because I saw you!'

Nora and Erin exchanged glances. 'You mustn't tell, OK?' Nora said.

'Cross me heart.'

'We're sewing new costumes,' Nora whispered. 'But we've got a custom in the family. A bit like wedding dresses, you know? *You can't see them until they're finished.* Nobody can. Otherwise…'

'Otherwise it's bad luck and the costume's ruined and you can't ever wear it and you have to burn it on a big fire,' Erin finished in a rush.

Lizzie shrugged. 'Could have just said so in the first place. Dunno why you and your ma had to be so ruddy secretive.'

'Ah well, families, y'know?' Erin grinned weakly. 'Hey! Speaking of our ma, you'll never guess what we found at the bottom of the bellybox.'

Nora produced a huge book as thick as a family Bible, with bits of paper poking out from between the leaves. 'It's her old scrapbook!'

'This goes back to before any of us were born,' Erin said proudly. 'Ma travelled with loads of circuses before Fitzy's. She kept souvenirs from all of them.'

The book was crammed with old handbills and

crackly folded posters, the colours still bright. In between, newspaper clippings had been pasted. Lizzie sat with the book on her lap and leafed through it eagerly. Nora and Erin sat on either side, pointing at the headlines and the pictures.

'That's Princess Caraboo!' Erin said. 'She was one of Ma's friends. She wasn't really a foreign princess, she was just a servant girl, but she fooled all the toffs.'

'Look at this lot!' Lizzie said. 'Samson, the world's strongest man. Thundering Cloud, the Indian chief, and his Tomahawks of Peril. Mister Marvel, the conjuror king, assisted by the mysterious Scheherazade. Here he is again – Mister Marvel, the Modern Merlin.'

The engraving showed a man in a Chinese silk hat, with a long moustache and a pigtail. He held a dove perched on his outstretched finger, as if he'd just produced it from thin air. 'The mysterious Scheherazade' looked on in a spangled mask, holding up her hands in what Lizzie thought was meant to be astonishment.

'Was he really Chinese?' Lizzie wondered.

Nora laughed. 'Of course not. It was all just an act. Ma said he was a handsome young chap under the make-up, though.'

'There's Ma!' Erin pointed at an engraving of a young

woman in a fringed buckskin jacket, firing pistols from the back of a pony. '"Desperate Deborah of Dublin, the Irish Hell-Cat!"'

'Blimey,' Lizzie said.

'Pa always said she was a wild one,' Nora said with a grin. 'Bet you never knew she was *that* wild, eh?'

As she headed back to her caravan, Lizzie caught sight of Lady Susannah striding angrily towards her with Fitzy in tow. There was no chance of ducking away and hiding. She'd been seen.

'There she is!' Lady Susannah marched up and jabbed a finger at her. 'I warned you I'd speak to your employer, girl, and that was no idle threat!'

Lizzie braced herself. She knew she ought to apologize, but she hated the thought of saying sorry when she'd done nothing wrong.

'Lizzie, we need to sort this out,' Fitzy said, while Lady Susannah folded her arms and glared at her. 'Her ladyship is quite upset.'

'You should have heard her,' the lady said. 'Making up the most outrageous stories just to see the frightened look on my face. I don't call that harmless entertainment, do you?'

'Well, Lizzie? What's your side of the story?'

'I weren't trying to scare her, I promise!' Lizzie protested. 'I saw danger in her future, and I was trying to *warn* her.'

'I see.' Fitzy tapped the side of his nose, thinking. 'I'm sure you meant well, but you can understand why she'd be upset, can't you?'

'I s'pose,' Lizzie admitted. Lady Susannah's stubborn refusal to take her seriously was giving her a headache. It wasn't Lizzie's fault if the warning scared her. The silly woman's life was being threatened. What was Lizzie supposed to do? Spell it out with flowers?

Fitzy was already ushering Lady Susannah away. 'Palm-reading is not an exact science. Sometimes one is told things that are *symbolic*, not literally true.'

'Symbolic?' the lady said, taking his arm.

'Like in a dream. If you dream of an angry dog, it doesn't actually mean anything to do with a dog…'

Lizzie watched, smouldering, as Fitzy led Lady Susannah towards the penny gaffs. He probably thought a visit to the Lobster Boy and the Bearded Woman would take her mind off the scary reading she'd had.

'I ain't a liar,' she muttered, clenching her teeth. 'And what I saw weren't symbolic, either.'

Yes, that was what galled her the most. It wasn't Lady Susannah's shock and anger. It was the accusation of lying. If Lady Susannah only knew the trouble Lizzie took to tell people the truth, instead of the comforting lies they wanted to hear…

She marched into her caravan and slammed the door. She thought of Lady Susannah's flushed, angry face. Then she remembered the sight of her in the vision, as she pleaded for mercy. Sobbing, her mouth twisted in agony … it was frightening, all right.

'I've got to help her,' Lizzie whispered. 'Or she'll end up dead. And I'd never forgive meself.' She punched her mattress. 'But how can I help someone who just won't listen?'

CHAPTER 13

There were only minutes left until the show was due to start. Lizzie pushed thoughts of Lady Susannah out of her head as she changed out of her clairvoyant's robes.

It was a relief to be back in normal clothes. The day had been roasting hot and the evening ahead was likely to be tropical too. Sitting in those heavy robes was like being a sausage baked in pastry.

She took a short cut to the show tent, slipping behind the caravans and into an ornamental garden. The heat brought the scent out of the exotic flowers, and made her feel light-headed and dreamy.

Johnson jumped out from behind a bush. She

screamed as he lifted a shotgun and levelled it at her. 'Who goes there?' he barked.

Lizzie gasped for breath and felt her pumping heart. 'You scared the life out of me!'

The groundskeeper squinted at her and grunted. 'Oh. It's you. The circus girl.'

'Who the ruddy hell did you think it was going to be? Napoleon Bonaparte?' She scowled at him as a thought struck her. 'You better not be hunting our elephants with that gun, 'cause if you so much as touch them, Fitzy will have your hide.'

Johnson lowered the shotgun, breaking it open as he did so. 'Don't take that tone with me, missy. I'm on guard. That Maharaja might be a trusting fool, but I'm not.'

Slowly it dawned on Lizzie that having the grumpy old man and his gun hiding out here might be a *good* thing. At least he seemed to know Lady Susannah and the Maharaja were in some sort of danger.

'Who exactly are you guarding against?' she asked.

'I don't know yet,' Johnson grunted. 'But I know this much. If that man's daft enough to go parading his wealth about through the streets of Whitby, then invite the whole of the town to his castle, then he's only himself to blame if he's robbed again!'

'You think someone's going to try, don't you?'

'God knows there's enough folk hereabouts who don't care for him, and they'd love to get their hands on some of the wealth he insists on showin' off.' He patted his gun. 'Well, not while I'm about to let that happen. His money pays my wages.'

Lizzie saluted him. 'Jolly good. Carry on, that man.'

Johnson eyed her, unsure if she was taking the mickey or not. 'On your way,' he muttered.

Lizzie ran the rest of the way to the show tent. She felt some of the weight had been lifted from her shoulders, now that she knew the old curmudgeon was standing watch. He didn't want to see Lady Susannah come to harm any more than she did.

As she neared the red and white striped show tent, she saw all the crowds had already gone inside. Johnson had made her miss the start. Well, never mind – circus people could always go round the back.

She slipped in through a humble canvas flap, into the backstage area with its darkened animal cages and pasteboard scenery standing in wait, and went round towards the back of the audience stalls. Lizzie lifted the dividing curtain, saw the seats were packed with people and grinned to herself. Lady Susannah and the Maharaja were right in the very front row, watching the performance. Surely nobody would try to hurt either of them in front of all these people? There had to be thousands here…

Johnson was on guard outside with his shotgun. The show tent was packed. *Nothing bad can happen*, she told herself. So she settled down to watch for a while.

Parp! went a horn as Didi, the serious whiteface clown, stood stock-still with rice pudding dripping down his face. JoJo threw up his hands in mock horror. The audience roared. The other clowns capered and bumbled about while Didi chased them from one side of the ring to the other.

Lizzie laughed so hard her sides hurt. So far the show was going down brilliantly. The people of Whitby were acting like they'd never seen a circus before – and for all she knew, many of them hadn't.

All the hard work her friends had put in at rehearsal was paying off now. The Maharaja had a whole new set of routines to marvel at, and he was every bit as delighted as he had been in Oxford. Lady Susannah just smiled politely, fanning herself, draped in a lace shawl. Lizzie felt a bit sorry for her – she must have too much on her mind to enjoy the fun.

It was sweltering hot inside the show tent. No wonder Lady Susannah had her fan out. The air was growing stuffy, and the smell of so many people packed together – not to mention the circus animals – wasn't exactly pleasant. *Never mind*, Lizzie thought. Only a few more acts to go until the interval, then we can have cool lemonade with ice from the ice house.

'Thank you, ladies and gentlemen,' Fitzy called, raising his hands. 'Those were, of course, the clowns. And now, a very special treat. Please welcome those daredevil girls, the equestriennes without equal, two matching measures of pure poise and poetry – the astounding Sullivan Sisters!'

Erin and Nora went cantering into the ring and instantly stood up on their saddles, smiling and waving at the audience. Gasps rang out.

Lizzie stared. The twins had told her they were working on new costumes, but they were still wearing the same dresses they'd worn in Oxford. Maybe the new ones hadn't been finished in time. She decided to believe that, and ignore any more sinister explanations that might be creeping into the back of her mind.

Gurinder Bhatti stood up in his seat and applauded. 'Go on, girls! *Bravo! Bravissimo!*'

Each of the twins, as they passed by, gave him a curtsey from horseback. The Maharaja found that charming, and blew kisses to them across the sawdust. He didn't seem to notice Lady Susannah slumping lower and lower in her chair.

Lizzie watched closely. The lady fanned herself weakly, but it clearly wasn't doing enough to stop the suffocating heat. Maybe she'd misunderstood the vision of her choking to death? Perhaps this was the moment, and she'd just been gasping for breath? Maybe, as Fitzy had said, the vision was symbolic.

No – there had definitely been a rope round her neck. And now Lady Susannah was whispering something to the Maharaja, who looked sad but nodded and waved her off. *She must be excusing herself, so she can go and get some fresh air.*

Sure enough, the lady stood and made her way to the main exit. She staggered as she walked and had to steady herself against the backs of the seats. If Lady Susannah left the tent, she'd be exposed to whoever was out there, waiting to do her harm. She had to be warned. But if Lizzie tried to struggle through the audience and catch up, she'd never reach her.

Without thinking twice, Lizzie turned and ran. She sprinted through the backstage area, out through the canvas flap and around the edge of the show tent, leaping over guy ropes as she went.

Lady Susannah was hurrying across the lawn towards the castle. The fresh air must have perked her up, because she wasn't staggering any more. Lizzie rushed up to her, shouting as she went: 'Your ladyship! Are you all right?'

The lady spun around, saw Lizzie and let out a startled yelp. She tottered to a halt and pressed her hand to her forehead. 'The heat … it was too much for me. I am retiring to the castle for a rest.'

'You shouldn't be out here on your own! It ain't…' Lizzie paused, remembering how angry the lady had been about her violent visions. 'It ain't sensible, ma'am, what with your jewellery being stolen and all.'

'How kind.' Lady Susannah managed a smile. 'But you needn't trouble yourself. I promise, I shall lock my bedroom door and check under my bed for miscreants.'

Lizzie offered her arm. 'I'll walk you up there.'

The smile faltered. 'That won't be necessary. Now, run along back to your circus. You're missing the show.'

'I've seen it before,' Lizzie said firmly. She didn't want to miss the final version of Dru's seaside tightrope act – the thought of what might happen if she wasn't there to watch made her squirm – but Lady Susannah's safety was more important.

Lady Susannah heaved a deep, impatient sigh and took Lizzie's arm. 'Very well. If you insist on nursemaiding me, I cannot refuse. Not in my weakened condition.'

As Lizzie led the lady back to her bedroom, a feeling slowly crept over her. Malachy sometimes read her single-page 'penny dreadful' stories bought from the street vendors, and in those the victims would often report a 'feeling of being watched' just before a horrible crime happened.

Lizzie knew those stories were just badly written trash. But that was how she felt now, as the lady gripped her arm and they climbed the long avenue of stairs up to her bedroom. *It feels like we're being watched.* Lady Susannah's room was high up in one of the towers, but Lizzie insisted on walking all the way up there.

When they finally reached the room, Lizzie

understood why the lady would feel safe here. It was a wonderful, private haven, hung with mediaeval-style tapestries and smelling deliciously of lavender and herbs, with a grand high window offering a spectacular view over the gardens. A lamp, turned down low, was burning on the bedside table next to an abandoned copy of *Punch*.

Lizzie ran to the window while Lady Susannah settled herself on the bed. 'You can see all the way to the sea!' Lizzie exclaimed.

'Yes, you can,' the lady said wearily. 'Since you're here, would you be a dear and fetch my smelling salts? It's a little brown phial on the dressing table.' She closed her eyes and lifted her feet onto the covers, shoes and all.

Lizzie turned to the table with its huge arched mirror and stopped in her tracks. The table's surface was strewn with jewellery – pearl necklaces, silver chains, pendants of ivory and jade, all muddled up as if they were a child's playthings. Lizzie forgot to breathe. There, in the middle of the jewels like an egg in a baby dragon's nest, gleamed the Heart of Durga.

Lizzie was suddenly closer to the giant ruby than she'd ever been before. For a giddy moment, she thought she could feel a mystical heat radiating from it. If she put out her hand, she could touch that beckoning, faceted surface.

She could do more than touch it. She could *take* it. In the mirror, she could see Lady Susannah stretched out on the bed, her eyes closed. It would be a matter of seconds just to snatch up the huge jewel and pocket it.

Well, if this was supposed to be some sort of test, she wasn't biting. There was the little brown bottle of smelling salts, ridged down the side so you could easily feel for it in the dark. She picked it up and brought it over. 'Here you go, yer ladyship. A whiff of these will bring you round.'

'Just put them on the bedside table, would you?' the lady murmured. She didn't open her eyes.

Lizzie drew the curtains shut, darkening the room but for the lamp. Just for a moment, she remembered what it had been like to look after her mother, when she'd been slowly wasting away. That was one of many Rat's Castle memories she didn't dwell on often.

'Better put the lamp out,' she said. 'Dark and peaceful, that's what you need.'

'Leave it lit!' Lady Susannah snapped. 'Off you go now, girl. Run along. I need to rest.'

'I can sit and keep you company,' Lizzie protested. 'Just till the show's over, then the Maharaja can come and look after you…'

Lady Susannah sat up. 'What is the *matter* with you?' she said sharply. 'Is your head still full of that nonsense about murder and mayhem? Daggers in the dark, is that it?'

'I know what I saw,' Lizzie stammered. 'And I know you don't believe it – an' I can't make you – but it's still true! My visions are never wrong!'

'For heaven's sake.' The lady didn't conceal her disgust.

Lizzie felt like shaking her, she was so frustrated. 'It ain't up to me. The stuff I see, it *always* comes true! If I leave you alone, and something happens to you, it's my fault!'

'I don't know whether you're a fantasist or a half-wit, and frankly I don't care,' Lady Susannah yawned. 'Let me put it to you this way. Either you leave, or I shall have you sacked.'

'You can't do that.'

'Can't I? All I have to do is tell my Maharaja not to pay Mister Fitzgerald his fee unless you are sacked. He will have to get rid of you or face ruin.' The lady lay back down on the pillows. 'Close the door behind you.'

Lizzie's hand shook as she pulled the door shut. She stood in the hallway outside, clenching her fists and breathing hard, refusing to cry although Lady Susannah's words burned in her stomach.

'I'm trying to save your *life*, you stupid woman,' she whispered. 'One day you'll thank me. Yes you will. One day.'

She paused at a tower window and looked out across the darkening land. Evening was drawing in. She could see the sea in the distance. There was only one ship still in the bay. Lizzie wondered what it was doing out there, all by itself. Was that a white mist gathering around it?

Next second, her heart missed a beat as a green light shone from the lone ship. *It's the ghost ship – and it's closer to the shore than ever!*

The light flickered as she watched. Then it flickered again. At first Lizzie thought the lantern was swaying in the wind, but then it suddenly struck her that there was a pattern to it. Three flashes, then a pause, then three more.

She watched the light flicker rhythmically and wondered what it could possibly mean. A ghost with a message from beyond the grave? Or maybe it was something even more sinister than that.

In a sudden flash of certainty that filled her with dread, she knew her instincts were right. Lady Susannah *was* being watched – and something terrible was going to happen to her. But she couldn't stay here and guard her, not without ruining Fitzy's Circus.

CHAPTER 14

As Lizzie headed back to the show tent, with the moon rising over the distant moors, she heard Ma Sullivan calling her. 'Lizzie! Need to borrow you for a minute.'

Ma had set up a long row of tables, with glasses and teacups borrowed from the castle and the water-boiler borrowed from the tea tent. 'Interval in five minutes,' explained Ma Sullivan, 'and that lot inside are going to want refreshments. I need an extra pair of hands.'

Lizzie couldn't very well say no. So she made tea and poured out glasses of lemonade clinking with ice, ready for the crowd, while craning her head round to get a look at the front of the castle in case some shadowy figure came sneaking up to it.

'Keep your mind on the job, Liz,' Ma Sullivan scolded her. 'Here they come.'

Any chance of watching the castle vanished as a horde of excited people burst out of the tent, chatting among themselves:

'Did you see the way he caught her? Like something out of a pirate adventure…'

'Daddy, did you see the elephant? Did you, Daddy? Daddy there were elephants…'

'Ooh, that lad, though, the French one … he can tightrope into my room any time!'

Lizzie forced herself to smile and greet people politely. For the next ten minutes, she worked hard serving refreshments and taking money from the grateful Whitby crowd. Eventually, the Maharaja himself came in for a glass of lemonade. He tipped her an extra shilling and stood by the stall chatting to the townspeople.

Lizzie did her best to eavesdrop, but he was just talking about the show. The first half had gone down well, by the sound of it. Maybe the locals would warm to him now, as he'd hoped. Although the kind of person who would throw a rock at you wouldn't be likely to change their mind over a night at the circus, would they?

'How's her ladyship?' Lizzie asked him when the crowds finally began to ebb. 'She looked a bit peaky. Someone ought to check on her.'

The Maharaja drained his glass. 'You're quite right. She'll probably be asleep, and I'll get a flea in my ear for disturbing her, but better safe than sorry, eh?'

'Better safe than sorry,' Lizzie echoed.

The gong sounded, calling the audience back inside for the second act. Fitzy stood in the retreating tide of people, looking very proud of himself. He sauntered over to the stall where Ma Sullivan and Lizzie were mopping the sweat from their faces.

'Done all right?'

'You're a sly old devil, Fitzy,' Ma Sullivan said. 'The Maharaja's holding a free circus, and you go and charge people for drinks on the lawn outside.'

Fitzy helped himself to a glass without paying. 'I can't very well give 'em away for free, can I? Besides, we're at the seaside. People expect to pay a little extra for their treats. All part of the fun.' He frowned. 'Speaking of paying, where's our patron?'

'Checking on her ladyship,' Lizzie explained. 'She

had a fit of the vapours and had to go lie down.'

Fitzy checked a pocket watch. 'Well, we can't start the second act without him. He's the reason we're here.'

'There he is!' Lizzie pointed.

'Something's wrong,' said Fitzy.

The Maharaja was running. His arms and legs pumped like pistons and his shirt-tails flapped behind him. He grabbed hold of Fitzy like a drowning man clutching at a rope. 'She's gone!'

'My good man, calm yourself.' Fitzy's voice was pure authority. He took the Maharaja by the shoulders and looked right into his eyes. 'Tell me what happened.'

'Lady Susannah,' blurted the panicking man. 'She's been kidnapped. Taken from her bed. Everyone warned me about the Whitby curse and the ghost ship, but I dismissed it all as superstition…'

'She couldn't have just gone for a walk? To get some air?'

Gurinder Bhatti shook his head. 'Her jewels are gone. There were dozens … whoever took her has stolen them too.' His voice rose to a wail. '*The Heart of Durga has been stolen! And my true love abducted!*'

'Oh Gawd, no,' Lizzie said in horror. 'I left her on her own.'

'You were the last to see her?'

'I wanted to stay and watch over her – I tried. But she wouldn't let me. She forced me to leave!'

'So why did you think she needed protecting, eh?' Gurinder Bhatti brandished an accusing finger. 'What did you know that you're not telling me?'

A gunshot rang out, echoing across the gardens. The Maharaja jumped. He glanced around, but there was no sign of an attacker.

'It came from over there!' Fitzy said.

'Johnson,' Lizzie gasped. 'He was guarding the castle with his shotgun. He must have seen someone.'

Fitzy set off at a run, and Lizzie and the Maharaja sprinted along behind him. Lizzie had the sinking feeling that they were too late. They'd find Lady Susannah's lifeless body sprawled in Johnson's beloved gardens. Or maybe she'd be found dangling from a tree. That rope around her neck in the vision could have been a noose…

They found Johnson holding his gun like a one-man firing squad. One of the barrels was still smoking. He was pointing it at Hari, who was pressed up against a tree, shaking with fear.

'Don't shoot!' shouted Lizzie.

Johnson didn't turn around. 'Had to fire into the air to get your attention,' he said gruffly. 'Tell the Maharaja to get over 'ere. I've caught that boy again.'

'I am here,' yelled Gurinder Bhatti, 'and we do not have time for this!'

Fitzy was livid. 'Johnson, what are you playing at? Don't you know what's happened?'

'Eh?'

Lizzie wanted to slap Johnson in his stupid jut-jawed face. 'Lady Susannah's been kidnapped, her jewels have been nicked, and you're still persecutin' Hari?'

'He's mixed up in this, whatever's going on!' Johnson insisted. 'I saw him sneakin' out of that big tent and scurrying about in the gardens. He'll soon tell what he knows, if you let me beat it out of him.'

'That won't be necessary,' Fitzy said. He gripped Johnson's arm and forced the shotgun down until it was pointing at the ground. Lizzie hadn't known he was so strong – or so brave. 'Hari, explain. Quickly, now. What were you doing out of the show tent?'

'I went to the ice house,' Hari stammered.

'Why?'

'The animals were overheating. I thought if I put ice in their drinking water, it would help cool them down.

See?' He lifted a bucket full of ice chunks.

'Let the boy go, Johnson,' the Maharaja said. 'Now, Miss Brown, I beg you, tell me everything you know. My fiancée's life may be in your hands.'

Lizzie quickly explained what she'd seen in her visions: the laughing man about to plunge a sword into Lady Susannah, and the hideous image of the lady tied up and begging for mercy. 'I tried to warn her, Fitzy,' Lizzie finished. 'You know I did.'

The Maharaja flailed his hands in complete despair. 'But who would do this to her? She must have had enemies – someone from her past.'

'And she never told you?' Lizzie asked.

'Never. She did not like to speak of her past at all. She said that all that mattered was our future together.'

'Gentlemen,' declared Fitzy, 'we must act immediately. We have to assume her ladyship is still alive, otherwise we would have found her body by now. I expect her abductor is holding her hostage, to give himself insurance as he makes his getaway.'

'Yes!' Gurinder Bhatti exclaimed, though Johnson looked grim and doubtful. 'Saddle up. We will give chase. Johnson, you search to the west, in case they have taken the road towards the moors. Fitzy, come with me on the coast road. The kidnapper may be making for the harbour.'

'What about the second half of the circus?' Lizzie said. 'It'll have to be cancelled!'

'Not a chance,' Fitzy answered, with a determined look in his eye. 'It'll be easier to hunt the villain down if most of the townsfolk are kept here. But the circus does need a ringmaster ... Hari, take a message for me.'

'To Malachy?'

'That's right. I think you know what to say. Gentlemen! To the stables!'

As the three men ran to fetch horses and Hari ran to deliver his message, Lizzie stood alone on the lawn, looking forlornly up at the castle. Somehow, despite her best efforts, some evildoer had crept inside and made off with Lady Susannah.

A cold chill gripped her heart. What had Elsie said about the ghost ship? When it came to harbour, the old legends said, it made off with a living soul. Johnson was local to Whitby. He knew the stories, just like Elsie did. No wonder he'd looked doubtful – he never expected to see Lady Susannah alive again.

Perhaps the shadowy abductor wasn't someone from her past, but from the world of the drowned dead?

Lizzie thought of the hooded figure standing at the helm of the ghost ship, with two bright gleams in its hood. As she did so, a shivering feeling crawled over her whole body. A vision was coming. A powerful one.

Hari came running back from the show tent. 'Can you believe it? Malachy's going to be ringmaster for the second half! He's been waiting all his life for this ... wait, what's wrong?'

'Havin' a vision,' Lizzie croaked. Like a woman in the throes of a fit, she twisted and shuddered – and found herself staring out to sea.

The crystal-clear vision showed the future. Lady Susannah was alive, but fighting for her life. There were cobwebs in her hair and her lovely face looked terrified. She was on a small boat, trying to fight off someone Lizzie couldn't see clearly.

Lizzie fell, gasping, to her knees on the soft lawn. 'They're headin' to the harbour,' she panted. 'He's going to take her out to sea on a boat, then kill her.'

'Probably planning to dump her body overboard,' Hari said darkly. 'Where are they now?'

'I dunno. But they aren't on the boat yet, because that vision was definitely in the *future*. So there's still time to stop him!'

CHAPTER 15

'Fitzy and the Maharaja are already riding down the coast road,' Hari said. 'They'll catch him for sure.'

'No they won't.' Lizzie knew it for certain. 'They haven't gone down the coast road. I know exactly where they've gone.' She ran to her caravan to fetch a lantern, with Hari tagging behind looking confused.

'But the only other road runs towards the moors,' he said. 'They can't have gone over open ground, surely? They'd be seen!'

Lizzie lit her lantern. 'They went *underground*. The old smugglers' tunnel.'

Hari's mouth fell open. 'How do you know?'

'The vision. Lady Susannah had cobwebs in her hair. And how else could they get down to the harbour quickly without being seen? Come on!'

From inside the show tent, the band struck up an opening fanfare. Lizzie could hear Malachy shouting, sounding clear and confident above the music. He was introducing Mario the Mighty, and the crowd applauded loudly.

Good luck, mate, she thought. *You can do this. It's in your blood.*

Lizzie and Hari ran from the warmth and festivity of the castle grounds out into the growing darkness of evening. The wind tasted of rain, and distant thunder trembled across the moors. The weather was hot, humid and close, and a storm was brewing to blow the lid off it all. From the way the goose pimples rose on Lizzie's arms, she knew it was coming soon.

They ran past the gates and down the road to the waiting clump of trees, which held shadows in amongst their boughs like thick webs. Lizzie had to use the lantern to find the old brick-lined opening.

'Here it is,' she told Hari. 'The Rum Road.'

'Look!' Hari pointed at a torn scrap of lace from Lady Susannah's shawl, caught on a low-hanging branch. 'You were right.'

Lizzie led the way down, holding the lantern high, while Hari nervously followed. Tree roots had come down through the roof of the tunnel and encircled it like tentacles. In the unsteady light, they seemed to move, as if they were about to stir into life and grab the children.

'Can you smell that?' Hari whispered.

Lizzie could smell lots of things down here – earth, old dead leaves, the damp musty smell that long-abandoned things have. Then she caught a trace of what Hari was talking about. A bitter, sulphurous smell.

'Gunpowder,' she realized, then added, 'Malachy smelled it before.'

'Maybe someone's planning to blow something up. Like Guy Fawkes.'

'It better not be this tunnel. One good sneeze would bring this lot down on our heads.'

Hurrying down the tunnel wasn't easy. Lizzie knew they were racing against time, but she didn't dare rush. Horrible fates kept arising in her mind. She saw herself stumbling, falling and smashing the lantern, leaving the two of them trapped in never-ending darkness. Or blundering into a support beam and bringing the ceiling crashing down on them with a roar and a rattle of falling earth.

'How long is this tunnel?' Hari asked in awe, when the exit was still far ahead.

'Half a mile, Malachy reckoned.'

Lizzie reached a turning she remembered, where Erin had pretended to be an undead smuggler chasing them through the musty dark. It was hard to believe this tunnel had echoed with happy laughter only a day before. Now it felt more haunted than ever.

'It is fascinating,' Hari marvelled, 'to think there is a secret path, hidden in plain sight.'

Something was nagging Lizzie, and she had to get it off her chest. 'I wasn't sure if you were going to come.'

'Why? I'm not frightened of cramped spaces.'

'But you don't like the Maharaja much, do you? Yet here you are, helping him get Lady Susannah back. And his jewel too.'

Hari stepped carefully over an ancient shard of wood with a rusty nail in it, lying on the tunnel floor. 'I don't want Lady Susannah to get hurt,' he said quietly. 'Keeping her safe is what's important. What I think of Gurinder Bhatti doesn't matter.'

When they finally reached the end of the tunnel and

opened the outhouse door leading into the yard of the Whitby Oyster, silence greeted them. No noise came from the pub, nor from the streets beyond.

The two of them made their way down into the town. All around them, windows were dark and doors were shut. Traces of mist hovered in the air and Lizzie glanced in at silent parlours and empty sitting rooms where no fires burned in the grates. It was as if the whole town had been spirited away, its inhabitants turned to wisps of fog that dispersed on the sea breeze.

'They're all watching the circus,' Hari said.

'None of them have a clue what's going on,' Lizzie agreed. As she listened, she was sure she could hear distant music and cheering carrying on the night air. Then a rumble of thunder drowned it out. The storm was coming closer.

They hurried through the streets, past shuttered shops and shadowed back alleys where anything might be lurking, down towards the harbour. Boats were moored along the quayside at the river mouth, but nobody seemed to be on them. Lizzie's chest hurt with the effort of running, and Hari gasped as he ran alongside her.

Finally they reached the path above the beach. Lizzie

collapsed against the railing and looked out over the waves. There, looming out of a bank of mist, was the sinister shape of the ghost ship – green light shining from its bow, casting an uncanny glow over the water.

Lizzie narrowed her eyes. There was a second light alongside the first. It danced and swayed – a hand-held lantern, it could be nothing else.

'He's got her!' she yelled. 'Hari, he's taken her out to the boat!'

'We have to reach them,' Hari said. 'Maybe I could swim? They aren't too far out yet.'

Lizzie had a better idea. She pointed at Elsie's boat, tied up on the beach. But Elsie was at the circus, with the rest of the town, and they couldn't ask her permission. 'We'll just have to borrow it,' she said. Her legs ached from running, but she forced herself to dash down the stone steps, across the shingle beach and up to the boat.

Together, she and Hari pushed the little rowboat into the foaming surf, wading up to their knees, and climbed in. There was a tangle of netting in the boat's bottom, along with a couple of woven wicker pots. 'Sorry, Elsie,' Lizzie whispered as she trod on the net. 'Wouldn't be doing this if it weren't life or death!'

Hari took the oars and looked over his shoulder. 'That's the famous ghost ship, isn't it?'

'Yes.'

He sniffed. 'There's that smell again. Gunpowder. And something else, something sharp…'

'Never mind that, just row!'

Hari rowed hard. The little boat sloshed away from the beach and quickly closed in on the green light shining from the fog.

The closer they got, the clearer Lizzie could see the ghost ship … and in a sudden flash she realized the fog wasn't fog at all. It was a thick white smoke, and it was pouring from the ghost ship itself.

In that moment, she knew for certain it wasn't a ghost ship and whoever was at the helm was flesh and blood. The green light, the smoke, the smell of gunpowder … everything made sense in the same moment.

'Hari, he's using some sort of *fireworks*! It ain't a real ghost ship at all!' That explained why they'd smelled gunpowder in the tunnel, she thought. Someone had been storing fireworks there. But who?

A blue blink of lightning lit up the sky. Seconds later, the growl of thunder rolled out across the land and sea. The storm was even closer now. If it caught them on the open sea, the little boat would be helpless.

They had almost caught up with the other vessel. Lizzie could see the green flare burning and a figure standing behind it, dressed in a hooded robe. The light flashed off a pair of dark glasses.

That explains what I saw, Lizzie thought. *He's wearing dark glasses to protect his eyes from the light of the fireworks. This whole ghost ship was just a hoax ... a piece of trickery, like a stage effect. But why?*

Someone on the 'ghost ship' swore as he saw Lizzie's boat drawing closer. The green light suddenly went out, though the swirling fog-like smoke remained. The lantern light vanished a second later.

'Stop where you are!' Lizzie yelled.

The rowboat shuddered as it struck the side of the 'ghost ship'. Lizzie stood up, the boat wobbling beneath her feet, and peered through the smoke. It was bitter and seared the back of her throat. She could just make out two figures on the deck above, one holding onto the other.

She turned up the flame on her own lantern and held it up high. What she saw made her gasp in shock.

'*You!?*' she said. 'I don't believe it!'

Billy, the charming confidence trickster from the

beach, stood laughing at her. His hood was drawn back now, and Lizzie could see it was no more than a costume. He had his arms around Lady Susannah.

Lizzie's thoughts rushed back to the day of the circus parade. Poor Lady Susannah had needed Lizzie's help to rescue her from Billy and his oily advances. Clearly, whispering in her ear had only been the start. He was determined to make off with her.

'That's your plan, is it?' she snarled. 'Kidnap the lady, but make everyone think she'd been taken by the ghost ship, so she'd never be seen again?'

'You'd be amazed what the people around here would believe,' Billy sneered. 'Superstitious bunch of chumps.'

'Let her go!' Lizzie yelled.

Billy laughed. 'As you wish.' He unfolded his arms from around her waist. 'Your ladyship, do you want to leave with these children?' There was a nasty smirk on his face that Lizzie wanted to smack right off.

'Come on, quickly,' she urged Lady Susannah. 'Don't be scared.'

Lady Susannah took a hesitant step forwards. There was still a good three feet of water between the two boats. Lizzie held one of the oars out to her, so she could take it and pull them closer. Lady Susannah grabbed the oar, but to Lizzie's amazement she tugged it right out of her grip and gave a strange, harsh laugh. As Lizzie stared in surprise, the lady swung the oar like a club.

The paddle caught Lizzie in the face. Blinding pain made her eyes water and her teeth rattle. 'Ow!' she cried, her hand to her cheek. Black fireworks were going off in her head. She hadn't been belted in the face like that since escaping from Rat's Castle and her father's fists. Pain, betrayal and fear swamped her like a wave. She fought the urge to curl up in a ball.

Lady Susannah yelled at her – and her voice wasn't the posh, clipped tones of a highborn lady any more. It was a West Country burr. 'That'll teach you to stop meddling, you little freak!'

As Lizzie staggered in pain, the taste of blood filling her mouth, a vision rushed into her mind. She was powerless to prevent it. It was as if the blow from the oar had cracked her skull open.

Lady Susannah, in a spangled mask, was lying in a box done up like a Chinese cabinet. Only her head and feet could be seen, poking out of the ends.

Above her loomed Billy in a magician's costume, his

drooping fake moustache held on with spirit gum. He was brandishing a long, curved sword that shone brightly in the strange light from the coloured torches burning on the stage.

As the lady screamed theatrically and struggled, Billy raised the sword. 'Time to die, my pretty!' he laughed, and plunged the sword into the box right in the middle section. The audience gasped and applauded. Then he plunged two more swords in, while the lady kept up the screaming.

With a flourish, Billy whipped the swords out and opened the box to reveal Lady Susannah alive and unharmed. They took their bows to a storm of applause. A master of ceremonies came on stage, shook Billy's hand and called out:

'Ladies and gentlemen, give a big hand for Mister Marvel the Modern Merlin, and his assistant – the beautiful Scheherazade!'

CHAPTER 16

Lizzie couldn't have felt more of a fool. No wonder Ma Sullivan had thought she'd recognized the lady at the Maharaja's party. She *had*. Billy was the stage magician who'd once called himself Mister Marvel, and Lady Susannah was his assistant ... his accomplice.

'I got it all wrong,' Lizzie gasped to Hari. 'Lady Susannah isn't the victim here – she's the culprit!'

'Looks like the penny's finally dropped,' mocked Lady Susannah. Or Scheherazade, or whatever her real name was. 'To be honest, I thought you'd rumble me a lot sooner.'

'She did too,' laughed Billy. 'See, darlin'? I told you

the girl was nothing to worry about.'

'Set the sail, Billy. We're leaving.' The woman shoved with the oar, pushing the rowboat away and out of reach. 'Cheerio!' she said, giving a mocking little wave.

'No you don't!' Hari grabbed the fishing net from the bottom of their boat. He flung it hard and it opened in flight, falling around Billy.

As the man struggled to free himself, Hari caught the net's trawling rope and pulled it, tightening the net around the magician as if he was a shoal of fish.

Billy laughed, seemingly unconcerned. 'Smart move, mate. Did I mention I'm an escape artist?'

'My Mister Marvel can get out of a straitjacket in less than a minute,' Lady Susannah mocked. 'A fishing net won't pose too much of a problem.'

Lizzie glanced back at the shore. Fitzy and the Maharaja would hopefully have reached the harbour by now. With any luck, they'd see her lantern's light out at sea and give chase. You could see a lantern all the way from the castle, she remembered, from when she'd been thrown out of Lady Susannah's bedchamber…

Suddenly another piece of the puzzle fitted into place. She looked inland until she could just make out the castle tower, and a light glowing in Lady

Susannah's window.

'No wonder you didn't want me to put the ruddy light out!' she yelled. 'It was a signal, wasn't it? And he was signalling back to you from the boat!'

Billy smirked from inside the net. 'Clever little scheme, weren't it?' he said. 'What with that dopey Maharaja watching her day and night, I couldn't meet up with my Susie for a chat, could I?'

'I did miss you, my honey bear,' cooed Susannah in a soppy voice that made Lizzie want to throw up. She leaned her blonde head against his chest. 'Of course, I did slip away once in a while…'

'I saw you on the beach together!' Lizzie fumed. 'Canoodling like a pair of lovebirds!'

Billy chuckled. 'And that daft Indian duffer thought my beautiful Susie was in love with him. With him! How naïve can you get?' He began to wrestle with the net, while Hari struggled to hold him fast.

Lizzie glanced back at the beach again. Lights were approaching on the coast road – the search party! But Billy could sail away at any moment, once he was out of his net. There was only one thing for it. *Billy loves to talk. That's his trademark. If I can just keep him boasting for a while longer…*

'There's one thing I don't understand,' she said. 'What really happened to your jet necklace?'

Billy tapped his forehead. 'You're not very bright, are you? Susie nicked it herself, and I flogged it!' He wriggled his shoulders, and the net continued to slide off him like a snake shedding its skin.

'So what happens now? You're just going to disappear, are you?' Lizzie yelled.

Billy clapped slowly, mocking her. Lizzie, with a start, realized that he'd got his hands out of the net.

'When the ghost ship steals a person away, they're never seen again,' laughed Susannah. 'Pretty convenient, don't you think?'

Out of the corner of her eye, Lizzie noticed that the search party had boarded a boat and were heading towards them. *I just need a little more time*, she thought. *Play to his vanity, keep him talking.*

'How'd you pick the Maharaja as a target, though?' she asked.

Susannah rolled her eyes. 'Flamin' heck. She don't ever shut up, does she?'

'He came to our music-hall show,' Billy boasted. 'He's a wide-eyed child, that one. When we saw him bouncing about in his seat, we figured he was soft in the head. Ripe for the picking, like. So me and my sweet Susie decided to take him for all he was worth.'

'Your sweet Susie,' Lizzie said, practically spitting the words out. 'You would have let her marry another man?'

'Oh, they wouldn't have been married long,' Billy mocked. 'Just long enough for Susie to siphon off every penny of his cash.'

'And then, when he was no longer useful?' snarled Hari.

Billy let out an ugly laugh. 'He might have vanished without a trace one night. Spirited away by the ghost ship! Never seen again, unless he was washed up on the shore.'

'But the famous Lizzie Brown told me we'd never be married,' Susannah spat. 'I could tell your reading was true. So we went to Plan B.'

'What's Plan B?' yelled Lizzie.

With an angry flourish, Billy flung the net away from himself like a cloak. 'Getting our hands on this beauty.' He dug in his pocket and held up a glittering red object almost as big as his fist. 'This ruby's going to make us both rich.'

'The Heart of Durga,' Hari gasped. 'That's not

yours to sell!'

All the struggling with the net had pulled the boats closer together until they were almost bumping. Hari jumped, catching hold of the edge of Billy's boat and heaving himself on board.

'Get out of it!' screeched Susannah. She aimed a vicious kick at Hari's face, but he nimbly dodged out of the way and crouched, glaring at her. She moved between him and Billy, blocking his path to the ruby.

'Give that back,' Hari hissed.

'Don't you lay a finger on me,' she warned. 'I'll show you how dirty a woman can fight.'

Hari tried to dash round her, but she grabbed him, ripping his shirt. He shoved her away. As they grappled, Lizzie had a flash of *déjà vu* – I've seen this before in my vision!

In the vision, Lizzie had thought Susannah was fighting for her life. She was on a small boat, trying to fight off someone Lizzie couldn't see clearly.

It was Hari. Lizzie had thought Susannah was being murdered. Her vision was coming true, but it wasn't what she'd thought it was at all.

With a yell, Hari gave Susannah a mighty push and sent her sprawling across the deck. Billy staggered backwards, still holding up the ruby, but now fumbling in his pockets for a knife.

'You ought to be afraid of me, boy!' he shouted.

'Some of his best friends are lions!' shouted Lizzie. 'You think he'd be scared of *you*?'

Hari dived at Billy and caught him round the waist in a flying tackle. Billy toppled backwards, his arms windmilling wildly. To Lizzie's horror, the ruby flew out of his hand, landed on the deck and went tumbling across it.

'No!' Hari yelled.

Susannah scrambled after the jewel like a cat chasing a woollen thread. She was too late. The precious ruby rattled and bounced across the boards like a great glass doorknob, then flew over the side of the boat.

Lizzie didn't pause to think. She moved by sheer instinct alone. She swung her arms and jumped from the boat. Her hands reached out for the jewel.

She snatched it out of the air. It felt so strange in her grasp, heavy and cool as an apple, covered with smooth facets. Next second, she hit the water.

She was in over her head, swallowed up by freezing darkness that bit her to the bone. The shock of it almost paralysed her. Out here, there was no sandy sea bed to put her feet down on. The water was deep enough to swallow a tall-masted ship.

But this time Lizzie didn't panic. Despite the intense cold, she knew what she was doing. She dog-paddled hard, clutching the ruby in a fierce grip, until her head broke the water. Puffing and gasping, she swam back towards the boat.

'That's it, Lizzie! Keep going!' It was Hari's voice. She saw him leap from the 'ghost ship' back into Elsie's little fishing boat. He held out his hand, and the sight filled her with fresh confidence. *I can do it. Hari knows I can.*

Susannah leaned over the edge of their boat, holding the oar menacingly. 'I'm going to smack her one, Bill.'

'Wait till she's in the boat, you daft cow!' Billy raged. 'If you put her lights out, she'll drop the ruby!'

'*What* did you call me?' Susannah shrieked.

'You heard!'

'After all I've been through for you?'

'You mucked it all up! If you hadn't had a ruddy palm-reading off her—'

'PUT YOUR HANDS IN THE AIR!'

The voice booming out across the mist was coming from a large rowing boat. Lizzie could see Fitzy and the

Maharaja, and a tall, stern-looking man in a black coat. He was holding a pistol. She took Hari's outstretched hand and gratefully let him haul her onto the boat. Meanwhile, Billy and Susannah slowly lifted their own hands as the police boat approached.

'You two are under arrest,' the policeman told them. He turned to Fitzy. 'I'm in your debt, gentlemen. We've been after these two for a long time.'

'What's the charge?' Billy bellowed.

'Fraud, conspiracy and robbery for a start,' the policeman yelled back.

Fitzy looked satisfied, but the Maharaja just looked heartbroken.

As the boat drew closer, Lizzie was sure she heard the policeman mutter, 'And you made me miss the circus, you ass. I had front row seats an' all.'

CHAPTER 17

The next morning, instead of leaping out of bed as usual, Lizzie lay dazed and half-awake as the events of the night before rushed back to her. It hadn't been a dream, she knew that. Her hair and the pillow beneath it still smelled of the salty sea.

Once Billy and Susannah had been taken into custody, Fitzy had rowed them back ashore. The Maharaja had draped his silk wrap over Lizzie's sodden shoulders, but it hadn't stopped her from shivering all the way. She remembered the terrible look of sorrow on his face.

'I've been a fool,' he kept repeating. 'Such a

stupid, lovesick fool.'

Hari, she remembered, had done his best to comfort the Maharaja. 'You mustn't blame yourself,' the boy had said, sounding more sympathetic than Lizzie would have expected. 'She was an actress. A highly talented one. She fooled everybody.'

Despite Hari's efforts, the Maharaja's gloom could not be lifted. Not long after everyone had returned to the campsite at Dunsley Castle, and Lizzie was drying off beside the little stove in the tea tent, Fitzy brought word that he had left town that same night.

'But where's he gone?' Lizzie had asked.

'He's on his way to London. To Buckingham Palace.'

'To see Queen Victoria?'

'Quite so. He may have his ruby back, but the poor fellow has lost the love of his life.' Fitzy had explained with a sigh. 'Naturally, the queen knows how that feels. She lost her husband Albert not long ago.'

It made sense. 'I s'pose they can comfort one another, then.'

Fitzy patted his pockets. 'He has paid us handsomely,' he said, 'and left orders for our onward journey. This has been most profitable for the circus and I do hope he manages to also put in a good word for us with the Queen...'

Now Lizzie lay under the covers, grateful that she wasn't under the sea at Fiddler's Green. She hoped Elsie could sleep safely now, in the knowledge that the ghost ship was nothing but a legend after all. Never again would that misty vessel return to haunt Whitby.

She yawned, stretched – and suddenly sat bolt upright in bed. 'Blimey!' she exclaimed. 'I almost forgot what day it is!' She pulled on fresh, dry clothes as quickly as she could, then dug under the bed to retrieve the shell bracelets she'd made for Erin and Nora. There was no paper around to wrap them in, so she popped them inside a velvet bag she sometimes used for her tarot cards. 'They'd better not have started their party without me,' she muttered to herself.

The castle lawns were shining with morning dew. All the caravans were quiet and there was no sign of life anywhere. Lizzie was all alone as she ran to the tea tent, bag in hand.

She burst in – and every single circus member was there to meet her, smiles on their faces. 'Happy Birthday!' they chorused as one.

'All together now,' Fitzy called out. 'For she's a jolly good fellow...'

Lizzie stood, smiling but bewildered, as the whole circus sang to her. 'And so say all of us!' they finished. 'Hip, hip, hurrah—!'

'Wait, wait,' she interrupted. 'You've got it all wrong. It ain't *my* birthday. It's Nora and Erin's birthday.'

'I think you'd better ask them about that,' Fitzy said, grinning. 'Nora? Erin? Let's be having you!'

The crowd of circus folk parted, as if this moment had been rehearsed – which, Lizzie realized with a shock, it must have been. Because there were Nora and Erin, holding a truly colossal cake, one twin on each side of it.

'It's not right that you've never had a birthday party,' Nora said, laughing at the look on Lizzie's face. 'And we just couldn't wait until your birthday, which is *months* away yet.'

'So you can share our party!' Erin declared. 'There are three names on the cake, not just two.'

Lizzie didn't know what to say. 'I brought you a present,' she told them quickly, before sheer happiness made her choke up. 'They're, er, both exactly the same, so you needn't fight over 'em.'

The cake was escorted off to a side table, while Nora and Erin put the shell bracelets on. 'Lizzie, they're beautiful!' Nora said. 'You must have taken ages over them.'

'I love mother-of-pearl,' Erin smiled. 'Goes great with me hair colour.'

'Girls, we have a confession to make, don't we?' boomed Ma Sullivan.

'Oh, yeah,' Nora said. 'You see, Lizzie, that time you came into the caravan and we said we were working on new costumes? That was a little white lie.'

'We were working on *this*!' Erin said. And she produced a hand-sewn bathing costume, striped with black and white, every bit as fine as their own.

Lizzie took it, laughing.

Dru sighed and shook his head. 'Does this mean the days of watching Lizzie run into the sea in her clothes are over? I will miss them.'

'I'll shove you into the sea in your clothes if you're not careful, mate,' Lizzie retorted, and everyone laughed. Her cheeks felt a little hot. All this attention was overwhelming.

'Right,' Ma Sullivan said, as if she'd read Lizzie's mind. 'It's a glorious morning, and I'm in no mind to sit around inside a stuffy old tent. There's a picnic ready, so let's go to the beach.'

Everyone gathered around the huge picnic hampers Ma Sullivan had packed. 'Looks like quite a feast, Mrs S.,' Rice Pudding Pete said, 'but it must weigh a ton! We're going to need to load up some of the wagons.'

'Oh, I don't think that'll be necessary,' Fitzy said with a twinkle. 'Hari, Zezete, did you attend to that little matter we spoke of?'

'The elephants are all ready,' Hari replied.

So it was that the cast and crew of Fitzy's circus went trooping through the castle grounds on their way to Whitby beach, with two elephants carrying the picnic baskets. This time, Lizzie got to ride on Akula and admire the splendid gardens from high above.

As they were nearing the great iron gates, Lizzie heard Hari mutter, 'Oh, *now* what does he want?'

Johnson the groundskeeper was lurking beside the gate, with a bucket in his hand. Lizzie braced herself for trouble, though at least he wasn't carrying his shotgun this time. But as they drew closer, she saw he was smiling. Stranger still, he was smiling at Hari.

'I picked these for you,' he said, showing Hari the apples that filled the bucket. 'From the castle orchards. I reckoned your elephants might like 'em.'

'Thanks,' Hari said. He looked very confused as he

took the bucket. 'They love apples.' *That's taken the wind out of his sails*, thought Lizzie.

'I was only trying to look after Dunsley Castle and its master,' Johnson said. 'But that don't excuse the rough ride I gave you.' He hung his head. 'I misjudged you, son. You're a brave lad, to do what you did.' He stuck out his hand awkwardly.

Hari looked at him. For a moment Lizzie thought he was just going to walk past with his nose in the air and leave the man standing there, looking stupid with his hand out. But Hari smiled too, and shook Johnson's hand.

Luckily, despite the sunshine, the beach wasn't too crowded. When the bathers and their families saw the elephants approaching along the coast road, they hurried up to see. The children's admiration turned to wild excitement when Hari led the elephants down the zigzag ramp and onto the beach. Ignoring their parents' warnings, the children came flocking up.

While Ma Sullivan busied herself with unpacking the picnic and laying out brightly-coloured rugs for the circus folk to sit on, Hari gently introduced the crowds of children to Akula and Sashi. Some of the braver ones reached up to touch the elephants, then jumped up and down on the spot squealing.

Eventually, some of the parents came and joined them. One hefty fellow with tattooed arms jokingly asked, 'How about letting my Bobby have a ride, then?'

'Of course,' Hari said, offering his hand. Young Bobby, in a sailor suit, stepped forward with his blue eyes very wide. Hari eased him onto Akula's back, clicked his tongue, and up went the elephant. Bobby clung on, whooping, while the other children danced around, out of their minds with excitement. 'Me next!' 'Giz a go on the other one, mister!' 'Dad, dad, I want one!'

A woman in a shawl sidled up to Lizzie. 'It were a lovely circus you lot put on,' she smiled. 'Haven't seen the like in years!'

'You'll come back, won't you?' her husband said. 'All of you?'

Once those two had said their piece, the floodgates seemed to open, and soon a crowd of grateful Whitby townsfolk was gathering to say thank you.

'Don't thank us, thank the Maharaja,' Hari pointed

out. 'This whole show was his idea. We wouldn't be here if it weren't for him.'

'Well, tell him thanks from me too,' said Elsie, nudging her way through the crowds. 'If you hadn't have come, I'd still be frettin' about that ghost ship.'

'How did you sleep last night?' Lizzie asked her.

To Lizzie's amazement, Elsie gave her a tight hug. 'Like a bloomin' log, thanks to you. I dreamed I met my brother again. When I woke up, I couldn't remember being so happy.'

Fitzy insisted Elsie stay for the picnic lunch. She sat next to Lizzie and the rest of the Penny Gaff Gang. Ma Sullivan passed around plates piled with sandwiches, salad, cold meats, grapes and bowlfuls of seafood.

'I can't believe that little minx Susannah had the gall to look me in the eye and act like she didn't know me!' Ma Sullivan said, lowering herself to sit beside Lizzie. 'I knew I'd seen her before. She and Mister Marvel toured with Kenroy's Circus for a while.'

'What was she like back then?' Lizzie was curious.

'Ah, she was a nasty piece of work. All the girls said she was no better than she ought to be. You've got to admit, though, they pulled off quite a sleight of hand.'

'Nearly pulled it off,' said Lizzie quietly, watching

the seagulls looping over the waves.

She thought of the palm-reading she'd given Susannah, and frowned for a moment. The vision of her future hadn't come true after all. She'd seen her weeping, her arms tied behind her back, pleading not to be killed.

Then the truth dawned on her. The vision she'd seen had been of Susannah in gaol, pleading with her gaoler to spare her the death penalty for her crimes.

No doubt Billy had been locked up too. *He might be an escape artist*, she thought, *but even he won't be able to escape from gaol.*

Fitzy point-blank refused to let anyone do any bathing straight after lunch in case they all got cramp and drowned, so with much protestation the circus children and Elsie were forced to sit and watch others splashing about for half an hour.

Lizzie noticed that Hari kept glancing at Nora, as if he was trying to work up the courage to say something. When she got a chance, she whispered to him, 'Spit it out, whatever it is, or we'll be here all day!'

Hari cleared his throat. 'Nora?'

'Mmm?'

'I thought you might like … that is, you said how much you…' Lost for words, he held out his hand. A necklace dangled from his fingers, small but beautifully crafted. Each faceted bead was glittering and black.

'Hari! That's never real jet?'

'It's real.'

Nora took it, handling it gingerly as if it were made of black ice, about to melt away in her hands. 'You great eejit, how'd you ever afford this?'

'Put it on,' Hari said, taking a step back.

'Not until you've told me where it came from!'

'I went gathering fossils,' Hari explained. 'The local jewellers sell them, so they took them in trade. I found some lumps of raw jet too, and sold them. Eventually I had enough money for a necklace.'

Nora smiled and fastened the necklace round her neck.

That's it! Lizzie thought. *That was the vision I had! I saw Nora putting on the jet necklace, only I thought it might be Lady Susannah's.*

Once again, her visions had all come true.

Erin folded her arms. 'So that's why you've been

acting so funny, is it? Claiming you had chores to do, then running off to the moors? All along you've been hunting for fossils and jet!'

'I wanted it to be a surprise,' Hari said. 'Sorry I had to mislead you.'

Nora ruffled his black hair. 'Ah, we never doubted yeh.'

I did, thought Lizzie. She smiled, admiring the lovely necklace, but inside she felt terrible. *I doubted all of my friends. I never should have done that. My visions might always come true, but they don't always mean what they seem to mean.*

'You can always trust your own crew,' Erin said with a sigh, looking over to the breakwater where Billy and Susannah had been sitting that day. 'I won't ever trust a performer again, though. They're all flash and dazzle, and they string you along and then break your heart.'

'Oh, I don't know,' said Malachy. 'They're not all bad.' He handed her a tiny parcel.

Erin eagerly unwrapped the gift and revealed a pretty silver thimble with the word 'Whitby' engraved in fancy script. She gasped with pleasure as the thimble gleamed in the sunlight. 'I can use it when we start working on our new costumes.' She winked at Lizzie, adding, 'For real, this time.'

Erin gave Malachy a quick peck on the cheek and he beamed brighter than a lighthouse. 'Thought you might like a souvenir of our visit to Whitby,' he said bashfully. 'It's been grand, hasn't it?'

Lizzie nodded in agreement and slowly grinned. *Malachy, you dark horse. You've had a crush on Erin all this time! I always thought you fancied one of the twins, and now I know which one…*

Dru patted his pockets. 'While we are giving gifts, I have *un petit cadeau.*' He passed Lizzie a shining silver comb with a flourish. 'Happy non-birthday. Every mermaid needs a pretty comb for her hair.'

Lizzie turned away to hide her blushes. 'Thanks,' she mumbled. Suddenly she felt hot all over, and desperately wanted to run into the sea. 'I'm going to change into me new bathing suit. My lunch must have gone down by now.'

Ma Sullivan laughed. 'I'd like to see anyone stop you, girl!'

Moments later, Lizzie went running out to the sea. She plunged in, feeling the cold sea all around her like a mother's embrace, and she began to swim with powerful, confident strokes. *I ain't afraid any more. I can swim!*

As she came up for air, treading water, she looked back at the harbour and Whitby Abbey overlooking it high on its cliff, beautiful as a painting. It seemed holy now, not haunted, with sunlight glowing from its ancient walls. Everything was as it should be.

She smiled, knowing she would remember her first birthday party for ever.

Read on for a sneak peek of the next
Lizzie Brown adventure, THE FAIRY CHILD...

CHAPTER 1

Malachy Fitzgerald leaned on his walking stick and stared at Lizzie Brown in disbelief.

'You mean to say you've never heard of King Arthur?'

'I've heard of Queen Victoria,' Lizzie said with a shrug. 'She's the one we've got, and that'll do for me.'

The two children were halfway up the path that threaded up the side of the spectacular mountain called Arthur's Seat. Overlooking the city of Edinburgh, it humped against the skyline like a sleeping dragon.

Lizzie looked down the way they'd come. She could still make out the red and white shape that was the show tent of Fitzy's Travelling Circus, standing out among the green of Holyrood Park. The caravans, including her own, were huddled in a cosy group behind it, as if to keep the chill October winds at bay. Her nose tingled from the sharp, cold air.

It had been a long journey to reach the Scottish city, and after spending hours jolting along in the back of a caravan, the circus folk wanted nothing more than to shoot off and explore the new site. But the work of setting up always came first.

Fitzy, the owner and ringmaster, had a kind heart but wouldn't tolerate slackers. 'A circus is like a pyramid of elephants,' he had told Lizzie once. 'We all stand on one another's shoulders. It only takes one person to slack off, and next thing you know, it's raining elephants.'

So the pegs had been hammered, the boxes unpacked, the animals corralled and the huge tent poles hauled into place, until the circus stood proud and ready. After that, the men were free to go and explore the pubs, while the women headed to the shops and the children did whatever they liked, so long as they stayed out of trouble.

Lizzie, the circus fortune-teller, and Malachy, the owner's son, were remarkably *bad* at staying out of trouble. When Fitzy demanded to know where they were off to, Malachy had told him: 'We're going to climb to the top of Arthur's Seat, Pop.'

'Any particular reason?'

'Best view of the city from up there.'

Fitzy had raised an eyebrow. 'All right. But make sure you're back here by three – I don't want to have to send out a search party because you two were off hunting the wild haggis or some such foolery.'

As they climbed up the mountain, it dawned on Lizzie that Malachy had another reason for wanting to reach the peak. The boy had a club foot, and though he used a walking stick sometimes, he refused to let his disability slow him down. He sometimes set himself physical challenges and forced himself to achieve them. Like this hike.

Halfway up, Lizzie had asked who Arthur was.

Malachy shook his head. 'I can't believe you've never heard of him. He was the legendary King of Britain, back in the olden days. Had a round table all the knights used to sit around ... Don't yawn, Liz, it's rude.'

'Don't sound like my sort of story, to be honest.'

'No? There's a witch in it. Bit like you!'

Lizzie laughed and shoved him playfully. 'Tell me about her, then.'

'Ooh, she was evil. Morgan le Fay, her name was. She tried to bring down the kingdom with her wicked schemes. She managed it, in the end, sort of. That's why there's only ruins now.'

'What sort of a name is Morgan Le Fay? Sounds French.'

'You're not wrong!' Malachy sounded impressed. 'It means Morgan the Fairy. I bet you thought fairies were just pretty little things, didn't you? Well, they aren't all like that. There's all sorts – dark ones as well as light. Ask Ma Sullivan ... why are you looking at me like that?'

'Because you're totally off your head, sunshine,' Lizzie scoffed, shaking her head. 'Bloomin' fairies. There's no such ruddy thing!'

'It's only a story. You don't have to blow your top over it.' Malachy strode past her without looking back.

She could tell he was struggling, but she knew better than to offer to help him. Now she felt bad for hurting his feelings. 'Sorry, mate. It's just ... there weren't no time for fairy stories back in Rat's Castle where I grew up.'

Rat's Castle was a sprawling London slum of narrow, filthy streets. Some families lived ten to a room, with nothing but a bucket for a bathroom if you were lucky, and no food except for what you could beg or steal. Lizzie thought any fairy that set foot there would shrivel up and die – if fairies had even been real, which of course they weren't.

Even when her mother had been alive, she had never told Lizzie fairy stories. Lizzie wondered why. Maybe she hadn't wanted to fill her daughter's head with the sweet lie of everything ending happily ever after. She had sung, though – old folk songs and street ballads. Those, Lizzie would always remember.

Her father's only stories had been about the drunken fights he'd got into. If he'd won, there would be boasts about how the man he'd beaten up was twice his size, but he'd flattened him with a single punch. If he'd lost, he'd spit out a bitter story about the other man's cheating or the treachery of his friends.

'I don't need fairy tales,' she told Malachy happily. 'Real life's magical enough for me, since I joined up with you lot.'

Fitzy's Circus had blown into Lizzie's life like a glittering tornado, whisking her up and out of the misery of the slums. Now she made her living as the circus's fortune-teller in residence, among larger-than-life characters more strange and wonderful than she could ever have dreamed.

In a way, she herself had become stranger and more wonderful than any of them. Because Lizzie had a power she didn't fully understand. All through her life she had glimpsed the future in her dreams, but it was only when she joined the circus that she learned how to use her clairvoyance to the full.

She was no sideshow fake, but a genuine psychic: the only one in the country, for all she knew. Just by touching someone's palm, she could see into their past and future. She could also speak to the spirits of the dead. Sometimes, visions would strike her without warning, as if some higher power was pointing her towards a wrong that needed to be set right.

She and Malachy walked on. He chatted about King Arthur's legend, while Lizzie admired the view. The mountain was bare, with only a few bushes and patches of scrub, but the sight of the wide open space still thrilled her – she was out of Rat's Castle's stinking streets for good.

'Come on, Lizzie,' Malachy said, wincing. 'We're nearly there.' He strode on ahead of her.

'It's not a bloomin' race!' she shouted.

The mountain's summit was a pitted crown of exposed rock. Malachy went to stand by the edge, shaking his walking stick in triumph, and for a second Lizzie thought he looked like a chieftain from the olden days, brandishing his spear at the city below.

She joined him and sat down on the rough rocks. The view really was as magnificent as they'd been told. Edinburgh was spread out far below them like a map brought to life. Lizzie imagined flying through the clouds like a witch, looking down on the beautiful labyrinth of streets and houses. There was the castle with its battlements and towers, brooding above the rooftops, somehow majestic and haunted at the same time.

'I'm glad we came here,' she said softly. 'I never dreamed I'd travel to a different country.'

'Scotland is beautiful,' Malachy agreed.

Lizzie let her gaze rove over the cityscape, following it round – and then she saw some factories in the distance by the harbour. Like an ugly scab on a child's face, they blighted the whole city. Tall brickwork chimneys stained with soot spewed out black smoke into the sky.

'I don't like them buildings, though,' she said with a shudder. 'They're like monsters. Devils, even. Chewing up everything around them, and belching out poison.'

Malachy laughed out loud. 'Listen to you! You sound like one of those reformists, handing out tracts in the street. "Improve working conditions! People before profits!"'

'But they're horrible! Look at them.'

Malachy stood and hooked his thumbs through his braces. 'That's progress, Liz. It doesn't always look pretty, but it's the future.'

Lizzie turned away. 'It ain't a future I want any part of.'

'Don't be soft,' Malachy said with scorn. 'Industry's a *good* thing. It's what makes this country strong. Rule Britannia and all that.'

'It stinks if you ask me,' said Lizzie, wrinkling her nose in disgust.

The two of them dragged themselves back to the circus camp, arriving worn-out and breathless with three minutes left to go. While Malachy went to help Fitzy prepare for opening night, Lizzie slipped into the show tent to watch the performers rehearse.

A little thrill of satisfaction went through her as she saw she hadn't missed the Astonishing Boissets. They were trapeze artists and high wire walkers – and young

Dru Boisset, at fourteen, was a rising star of the show.

Lizzie watched him walk from one end of the wire to the other with his sister Collette poised on his shoulders. 'Smile!' yelled their father, Pierre. 'I do not care 'ow much it 'urts. Always smile for the crowd.'

Dru smiled and waved to the empty seats. His eye caught Lizzie's, and his smile broadened, becoming real. Lizzie blushed and waved back, her thoughts suddenly in a muddle. Dru seemed to have a lot more muscles than he used to...

Without warning, Collette's smile faltered and became a grimace of pain. Dru seemed to sense something was wrong and hurried to the end of the rope. His sister climbed down the ladder, clutching her back and moving stiffly as a broken doll.

Better give them some privacy, Lizzie thought as the Boissets huddled together to talk. *Something's wrong, by the look of it.*

She went and found her friend Hari in the animal enclosure. Her eyes widened as she saw a furry little creature hopping about in front of Hari. 'Wait, is that a monkey?'

Hari flipped a raisin into the air. The monkey flung itself up, caught the raisin and began to nibble it. 'Lizzie, meet Hanu,' Hari said. 'He's the newest member of our circus menagerie.'

'Hanu?'

'Short for Hanuman – he's one of our Hindu gods. The monkey god.'

Lizzie knelt down for a better look. 'Can I touch him?'

'Of course you can. He's tame.'

Very gently Lizzie reached out and stroked the soft fur on the monkey's head. Hanu glanced up at her with beady black eyes. 'He looks like a little wise old man,' she said, enthralled. Then she jerked back in surprise as Hanu skittered closer. She locked eyes with Hari and kept very still.

The monkey tugged at the fabric of her skirt, then lifted himself up and settled in a warm heap in her lap. He blinked at Lizzie as if to say, 'I can sit wherever I like'.

'I love him,' Lizzie said. 'Wherever did you find a monkey up in Scotland?'

'He was a present from the Maharaja Gurinder Bhatti. To say thank you for the show we put on, and … for the other stuff.'

Lizzie knew exactly what 'the other stuff' was. The

Maharaja had summoned the circus to Whitby, in the north of England, to put on a show for the locals at his expense. But unbeknownst to him, someone close to him had been plotting to steal his prized ruby, the Heart of Durga. It had all been connected to the appearance of a mysterious ghost ship in Whitby Harbour.

The monkey bared his teeth and made a chittering noise. 'He wants to be fed,' Hari explained. 'He always wants food. Greedy little beggar. Here, you feed him.'

He passed Lizzie a date, and she held it gingerly and watched Hanu reach up to take it. They monkey bit, chewed, glanced around as if fearful some other animal would snatch his date away, and then bit again.

'Look at his little fingers,' Lizzie breathed. 'They're just like a person's.' Watching the monkey eat, she realized that she was starving too. She lifted Hanu out of her lap and set him on Hari's shoulder. 'You'd best stay here, little fella. If Ma Sullivan catches you in her tea tent, she'll scream blue murder.'

Ducking into the tea tent, Lizzie saw that her friends Erin and Nora, the Amazing Sullivan Twins, were having their dinner too. Their mother was outside, fetching more wood for the cooking stove.

'Did you make it all the way to the top of Arthur's

Seat?' Erin asked. 'Did Malachy?'

'Course we did,' said Lizzie with her mouth full. 'You can see all the way over the city. Come next time!'

'We can't,' Erin said, kicking the folding table leg. 'Ma won't let us.'

'"Climbing up a mountain? Are yeh mad? What if you twist an ankle, eh?"' said Nora, imitating their mother's Irish brogue.

'"What about your practice? We're not here for a holiday!"' Erin joined in.

'"When you break both your legs, don't come running to me!"' the twin bareback riders finished together, and burst out laughing.

'My ears are burning,' Ma Sullivan said darkly, as she came back into the tea tent. Erin and Nora instantly clammed up. But their eyes still twinkled with silent laughter.

Ma Sullivan had a saucer in her hand, and as Lizzie watched, she added little pieces of food to it. Then she turned to leave.

'Have we got another new animal?' Lizzie frowned. 'I haven't seen a cat around.'

'It's for the Good Folk,' Ma Sullivan said.

Lizzie looked blank.

'She means the fairies,' Nora explained.

Lizzie laughed, not sure if Nora was joking. 'Not you lot as well as Malachy! Am I the only person in the circus who doesn't believe in fairies?'

'Hush, now,' Ma Sullivan said sternly. 'There's more fairies in Scotland than anywhere else in these lands. If you look with your heart, and not just your eyes, you might be lucky enough to see one.'

Nora and Erin nodded. 'You'd best be careful, Liz,' Erin said. 'You've got to treat them right, the fairies. If you don't, they're liable to take it personal.'

'And that,' Nora said with a serious look, 'always means trouble.'

To find out what happens next, read
THE FAIRY CHILD

Don't miss the first book in

THE
MAGNIFICENT LIZZIE BROWN
series

Roll up, roll up! A hair-raising adventure is about to unfold!

Join Lizzie Brown, the fortuneteller's assistant, and her gang of circus friends, as they try to uncover the identity of the mysterious phantom.

In Victorian London, a masked figure has been thieving from houses and evading the police. When Lizzie Brown has a psychic vision about the burglar, she knows she has to act. But this phantom is proving to be more dangerous than a tightrope without a safety net...

Don't miss the second book in

THE
MAGNIFICENT LIZZIE BROWN
series

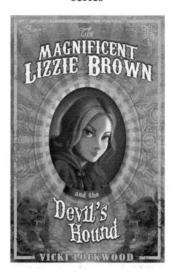

Something terrifying is circling the circus's new pitch.
The locals speak of a monster known to roam the nearby
cemetery. But Lizzie Brown doesn't believe it.

After a chilling message from beyond the grave and a
meeting with some mysterious criminals, Lizzie and her
gang confront the so-called 'devil's hound'. But they find
the story has only just begun…

For more exciting books from brilliant
authors, follow the fox!
www.curious-fox.com